Warmth from the Rising Sun

Shoju and Matashi, Book One

Kon Blacke

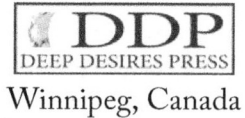

Winnipeg, Canada

Copyright © 2024 Kon Blacke
Cover layout copyright © 2024 Story Perfect Dreamscape

This is a work of fiction. Names, characters, business, places, events, and incidents are either products of the author's imagination or used in a fictitious manner. Any resemblances to actual persons, living or dead, or actual events is purely coincidental.

Editor: Margaret Larson

Published May 2024 by Deep Desires Press, an imprint of Story Perfect Inc.

Deep Desires Press
PO Box 51053 Tyndall Park
Winnipeg, Manitoba R2X 3B0
Canada

Visit http://www.deepdesirespress.com for more scorching hot erotica and erotic romance.

Subscribe to our email newsletter to get notified of all our hot new releases, sales, and giveaways! Visit deepdesirespress.com/newsletter to sign up today!

Warmth from the Rising Sun

Author's Note

This boy's love story contains graphic gay sex. It also contains fetishes such as shibari (rope bondage), cum and saliva worship, and vacuum cupping for titillation.

This story also falls under the boy's love Omegaverse umbrella, a genre where men can get pregnant. Omegaverse, even though unique to boys' love, can trace its origins back to Western sci-fi parody stories (fanfiction) and love stories between werewolves and humans.

For this story, I have done my own spin on the boys' love Omegaverse. In it, *all* the men living within the "secret village" can get pregnant—they are all Omegas. But like other stories in this genre, Omegas come into their monthly heat at which time they are then able to be impregnated to bear a child. They have a reproductive organ that functions similar to a uterus within the anal cavity, above where the prostate is located. Only boys are born.

All characters involved in any sexual act or sexual situation are over 18 years of age.

Enjoy Shoju and Matashi's story!

Glossary

Senpai (spelt sempai in Western) = mentor
Sensei = teacher
Uke = the receiver during sex/the bottom
Seme = the giver during sex/the top

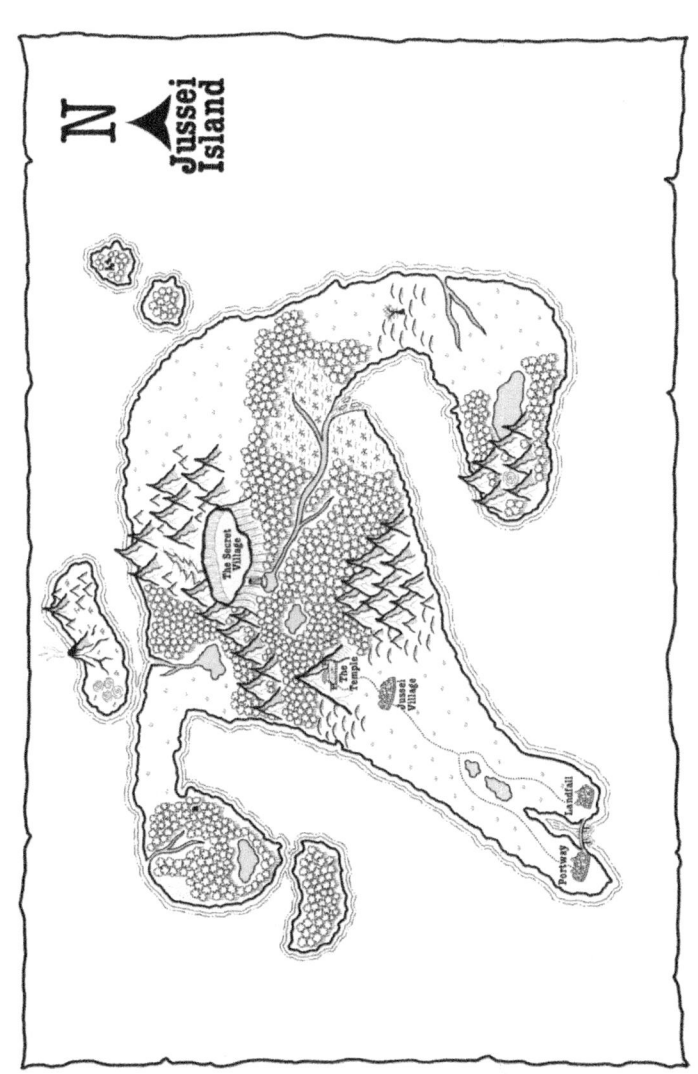

1

Shoju's mother beamed with pride while she fussed over his best outfit, something which involved picking off imaginary lint, then flicking it away, so it seemed. He was wearing a navy blue samue-style jacket with matching pants, divided toe socks known as tabi, and geta thong sandals; the outfit sure was the whole deal when it came to getting ready for what was about to happen.

He kind of felt good in it.

His mother's smile was infectious, and he couldn't help but smile, too. It was a happy moment, momentous even, and he was glad he could share it with her.

Although, she sure had to spoil it when—without a bat of an eye, mind you—she asked, "Now, Shoju, did you put your fundoshi on correctly this time?"

Shoju was taken aback. "Oh…my god, Mum! Really? I know how to put on traditional underwear, seriously." He realised she was doing that screwed-up face thing now. "And no, I'm not going to show you to prove it."

"Are you sure?" She clicked her tongue. "I can help you if you got it wrong. No shame in me doing that, is there?"

"As sure as I'm standing here." He shifted his weight.

"And I'm not six years old anymore, in case you hadn't—" He stopped himself, knowing he'd probably crossed a line then.

Today wasn't about disrespecting anyone, least of all his mother. More so because he *was* of age now. The man of the household, as it were, being the eldest and only son. He had to take that on board. And do so seriously, too.

As he thought about that more deeply, he remembered his eighteenth birthday celebration: a party that had lasted *all* week with the whole village in attendance, full of merriment and cheer done in the traditional way, complete with costumes, beating drums, crashing cymbals, and fireworks. What a spectacle! What a racket! Although the saké was even rougher on him, especially the hangover part afterward. It still felt as though his tongue had grown fur on it, even days later.

Shoju, therefore, decided to change tack with the conversation. "But you know I much prefer wearing normal undies. Fundoshi feel weird."

She smiled once more—a relief for him to see. "Oh, how so?"

At that, Shoju felt his cheeks warm even more, realising it was kind of embarrassing talking like this with his mother. So…openly. Not a normal thing to do. Then again, this wasn't a normal situation. As such, he decided to humour her. It was her day as much as it was his, in a way.

Probably more so.

After a swallow, he replied, "Because there's that bit between my butt cheeks that makes it feel weird, that's how so, Mum." He giggled, looking down at his feet as his discomfort increased. "And let's not even mention how I've gotta…you know…have my dick all upright and pressed against my body, not free and hanging down like how it's supposed to be. It just doesn't feel right, honest."

She snorted a laugh. "Oh, the problems you have, hey?"

"Tell me." He looked up to meet her stare. "Why do I have to wear it, anyway? It's not like anyone's going to see me in it…are they?"

A frown for a moment. "When you attend temple, especially today of all days, you'll wear it just like you're wearing all your other traditional clothing. All right?"

"Yes, Mum."

"There's a good boy."

But Shoju wasn't quite finished, seeing as everything seemed to be all out in the open now. "I don't see how it'll make a difference. It's not like my bulge is going to sway their decision, is it? Well…my lack of a bulge thanks to the fundoshi squashing everything down there, I mean."

She pressed her lips against Shoju's forehead, giving him a loving kiss like she usually did whenever matters turned serious. "It's an important day." Then she hummed while adjusting the material over his shoulder for the tenth time. "You've got to look your best."

"I know, I know." Shoju sighed. "But they still won't choose me, no matter what I'm wearing."

She stopped what she was doing to look him in the eye that time, her deep browns studying him, misting over, if he wasn't mistaken. "Now why on Earth would you say something like that?"

Shoju, under a different scrutiny, shrugged. "I'm not

exactly candidate material, am I? For a start, I'm not handsome or lean like all the other boys. And you know they only pick those kinds—"

"Nonsense."

He sighed again. "Mum, look at me. *Really* look, please. I mean, I'm not fat exactly, but I've got a bit of a gut and...and to top it all off, I've even got what they call 'man boobs.' If I lean over, they look like little tits...for real!" Another flush of embarrassment found Shoju.

He hated how he saw himself.

More often than not, such thoughts made him miserable, which then resulted in him eating more. Eating in excess put on more weight. Putting on more weight made him even more depressed.

A vicious circle, and one he found hard to break.

Impossible even.

"You simply have plump pecs, Shoju. Plump pecs and a full tummy, and that's all. And yes, you *are* handsome. Very handsome." She returned to her fussing, humming once more. "And besides, who you are on the inside should decide your fate, not how you look. You'll be chosen; I know it in my bones. You'll see."

"Um...what are you basing that on?" Shoju couldn't help smiling; her enthusiasm really *was* communicable. "Because you *can* see me, right?"

Mother harrumphed. "You're a kind-hearted, wonderful boy, and that's why you'll be chosen. How could they not select you for a temple position this season? And what's more, I bet you'll even be chosen as one of the honoured few because you'll be an asset to them, all studious and honest like you are."

"Wow." Shoju managed a giggle, even if his thoughts had begun spiralling. "If they selected on parental enthusiasm alone, I'd be a shoo-in."

"You already are."

He was about to disagree when there was a gentle knock on the front door. Shoju announced, "That'll be Mat—and in the nick of time, too."

She held her smile, an expression plastered on her this day…well, every day since his birthday party, he was certain. "Matashi is such a good boy as well; he really is."

"I agree. And Mat *will* be chosen because he's handsome, lean, and muscular instead of having a little too much padding, like me." Shoju would even bet Mat's bulge would still be something to admire even in an ego-crushing garment like a fundoshi.

But he didn't say that out loud.

Mother replied, "That's your bias talking because Matashi is your companion." She left Shoju standing there in the front sitting room while she went to the door to answer it.

"Oh, and you're *not* biased?" he called to her.

She waved her hand dismissively with a "pfft!" before greeting their guest with a forehead kiss and a loving hug.

Matashi squirmed under her attention, as always.

A heart beat later, he was standing in front of Shoju. Mat took Shoju's breath, he really did. So beautiful he was, all black as black hair, hazel-eyed, and with soft tanned skin accompanied by a gentle smattering of dark freckles over the bridge of his nose that got more prevalent as the summer wore on. He also had full, so-very-kissable lips, too.

For the longest time, they both took each other in, the tension between them palpable. Shoju's stomach went all queasy, his heartbeats fluttering.

He wanted Mat to be his first, no doubt about that.

Shoju, coming out of his infatuation for a moment, realised Mat smelled good, all fresh and clean and of honeysuckle and gardenia. "You…you went to the public bath first thing this morning, then?"

"I did," he replied with a husky voice once cleared.

"Sorry I couldn't join you." Shoju felt slightly dejected. "But you know how I feel about…being naked in front of others. What with me being…" His words then faltered on his lips, unable to be spoken as his throat tightened. Shoju found he was getting all emotional, everything becoming too much all of a sudden. Who could blame him for that, really?

"It's okay." Mat stepped closer, grabbing both of Shoju's hands to clasp them tightly. "I understand."

"I know you do, and I'm thankful for it."

"You know I love you no matter what, Shoju. How could I not? You complete me, honest."

"And you complete me, Mat."

A delightful moment of hesitation before they came together, lips pressed gently as they kissed. That was so much better. Shoju felt a tear fall when his knees weakened, as always when they shared such tender moments together. He loved being in the embrace of his companion, and he couldn't be happier…today of all days, as well.

Mat never saw him in any superficial way, either, because the love was always shared, unfalteringly and unconditionally.

Always.

"I hope we both get chosen," Mat offered once they'd parted, Shoju's lips tingling delightfully. "I don't know what I'd do without you, Shoju."

Shoju swallowed that lump down. "We both will, I know it."

"See," Shoju's mother chimed in, "that's the spirit!"

Shoju couldn't help but let out a guffaw at that.

Shoju and Mat walked hand in hand toward the temple, the moment of their kiss, full of love and belonging, of friendship held dear most of all, still lingering on his lips. He hadn't stopped feeling the warmth from it, like that of the rising sun permeating through every fibre of his being.

A wonderful feeling.

Pity his anxiety began to creep uncomfortably all through him the closer they got to their goal, the reality of what was about to happen finding him suddenly. He was glad he had Mat by his side.

Shoju was also happy his mum was with him too. She walked ahead with Mat's parents and younger siblings, all of them talking quietly, excitedly, as they made the long journey up the mountainside on stairs hewn by pick and axe from the rock centuries ago.

The morning was already warm, being the height of summer. Still, the clinging humidity kept the forests around the temple thick and full of life. Many times, Shoju spotted wildlife, from lizards and snakes warming themselves on exposed stones, to deer spying on them, to native birds squawking above as they walked below, upset they'd been disturbed by passers-by.

"I'm a bit scared, Mat," Shoju admitted.

"Why would you say that?" Mat stopped to look at Shoju. "There's nothing to be scared of."

Shoju shrugged. "Perhaps it's because I don't know what to expect. I always get like that when I don't know things."

"I know you do." Mat chuckled lightly, continuing their journey. "But from what I heard from my older brother, we'll have a tea ceremony, be asked a few questions, and then it'll be selection time."

A thought struck Shoju. "Your brother…he, um, wasn't selected, was he?"

Mat's expression turned sour. "No." He spat that word out like it was poison on his tongue.

Shoju knew it wise not to say any more.

Boys who weren't selected became outcasts; they weren't even considered men by the villagers after that. Most had to flee to the mainland if they were to scratch out any sort of living. Some even disappeared deep into the forest beyond the mountain's far-reaching shadow, never to return.

God knows what happened to them.

More than likely, they hadn't survived out in the wilds, Shoju imagined. He knew the wildlife wasn't the only thing to worry about beyond the walls of the main village and temple—some have told of strange supernatural beings who live in the great unknown.

He shivered all over at that thought, gooseflesh rising on his exposed skin, despite the heat already, making him even more tense. He shook his head, trying to rid himself of his anxiety, but not doing too a good job of it.

Shoju really was a mess of nerves and anxiety, that was for sure.

Mat must have picked up on that through their physical connection, shooting Shoju a questioning glance. "Let's try and keep positive," he offered, calmer than Shoju would have believed given the circumstances. "We'll both be all right, okay?"

Shoju knew being chosen meant a good life for him and his mum—the alternative was unthinkable. So much rode on what happened within the next hour or so that it made his stomach hurt. "Okay."

Behind them, eight other boys of age chosen by the village elders out of the many, many likely candidates walked with their families. All of them looked as nervous and desperately hopeful as Shoju felt, despite their quiet banter rippling through the hazy air in waves of enthusiasm and doubt in equal measure.

Before too long, the temple's gate—or torii, as it was known—loomed like a sentinel guarding heaven's entrance up here on the mountaintop. It was a massive architectural

wonder carved from wood by many expert hands eons ago. It was also painted garishly in bright crimsons and emerald greens.

A sight to behold.

To mark the importance of the day, many silk-made flags of all colours hung from the torii, fluttering and snapping from a breeze kicked up by the heating earth as the sun rose.

"This is it," Shoju whispered to himself. "From here, I'll either become a man or an outcast. No pressure, hey?"

Beyond the gate, the stone steps became smoother, the gardens manicured. The temple itself was a simple structure, not unlike the town hall of the village, but far more opulent with its detailing. In front of it, the temple masters stood, six of them, all dressed in their finest ceremonial robes, as Shoju and the rest of them were. Behind the masters stood the temple's servants and guards, equally impressive with their outfits and serene but sombre expressions.

A man with a wispy moustache as his most prominent feature—clearly the temple's leader as his outfit was more imaginative than everyone else's, with its lighter blues and its white trimmed highlights—took a confident step forward.

With a raise of his hands, he announced, "Welcome candidates to the selection. We wish you all the best."

The man bowed.

Shoju, along with Mat and the other eight boys, bowed in return.

The man continued, "My name is Master Fuoco, and

those boys who wish to put themselves forth for the ceremony that will follow presently, please step forward to announce yourselves."

Shoju, swallowing hard, stepped forward.

As did all the others.

Fuoco said, "The family members who have attended with their sons can remain within the gardens here. You'll all be looked after while we choose the boys who will become either servants, guards, or the honoured of the temple, as is our tradition." Shoju knew what that meant—the boys *not* chosen would be given no reprieve. They would be outcasts with no hope of any sort of future, for them or their family.

Panic began to rise within Shoju, and he squeezed Mat's hand tighter.

Mat reciprocated.

As if to reinforce his concerns, Master Fuoco added, "But no matter what roles the boys are chosen for, those who have been, will be treated with respect and honour—as will their families be. So, I thank you for your patience while we make this important decision."

He bowed again.

The families bowed that time, including Shoju's mum.

From there, Shoju was confronted by one of the other masters offering him his hand. "Come with me, please," he said with a soft, gentle voice, one that reflected his appearance perfectly.

"Yes, senpai." Shoju let go of Mat to take the man's hand. It was warm and welcoming and accompanied by a smile, one that fit so well on the master's lips.

Some of his nerves subsided, even if his anxiety heightened.

With Shoju being led toward a building beside the main temple itself, separated from the others, including Mat, the master then said, "My name's Master Horo, and I'll be the one who'll decide if you are chosen to join us. Please don't be nervous; just do as I ask of you and you'll be fine. Do you understand?"

"I th-think so," Shoju replied with a mild stutter. The nerves he thought had abated were nowhere near doing so, he realised.

He swallowed hard…again.

They approached a stone fountain before entering the building. "Please wash your hands and mouth in the sacred waters of the chōzuya, then we can continue in earnest."

"Yes, senpai."

The water was surprisingly cool and refreshing against his skin, no doubt pumped up from a natural spring deep within the roots of the mountain; he certainly tasted minerals on his lips. Once he'd cleansed himself in the proper way, which he did as thoroughly but as hastily as he could, they then proceeded without delay.

Master Horo smiled, seeming satisfied. Whether by what Shoju did or with Shoju himself, he didn't know. Couldn't know. All he knew was the man held his hand once more, leading him onward.

Shoju liked that.

The room of the building he was taken into was cosy. The tatami mats covering the wooden flooring in a carefully placed pattern were the first things he noticed—the smell of their comforting grassy but herbal scent hitting Shoju straight away, too. There was also a small brazier in the centre of the room, wisps of bluish-tinted smoke curling lightly from it. Other than that, the room was empty aside from a tray with a traditional tea setting upon it. Although, the feel of the room, so peaceful and serene, made it kind of feel like home to him.

Shoju missed his mum already at that thought.

"Please sit," Master Horo invited.

Shoju, crossing the room but ensuring he didn't step on the fabric edging of the tatami matting due to the protocols that would be required of him, finally sat cross-legged opposite Master Horo. He also straightened his back, giving the man his full attention, as would also be expected of him.

Horo began pouring the tea with practised ease.

The smoking brazier soon overtook everything else, including Shoju's attention. Whatever was burning within it made him feel kind of light-headed. Was it some sort of spice? Because it seemed to affect Shoju on a deeper level. Really relaxing him, he had to admit.

Bringing Shoju back to the moment, head spinning, Master Horo said, "Tell me about yourself, please, Shoju Fa."

"You know my name, senpai?" At that, Shoju imagined the man knew a lot more about him than he would have believed.

"I know a lot about you—you are a candidate, after all."

"Then what can I tell you that you don't already know?"

Master Horo smiled, knowing and warm at the same

time. "Tell me about your deepest desires." He offered Shoju the filled cup with both hands and a bow.

Shoju took it with the same ceremony. He soon sipped upon a nice oolong blend, fragrant as well as refreshing. "I don't know if I have any of those."

"Everyone has desires."

"My only desire is to be with Matashi," Shoju admitted.

A slight raise of an eyebrow at that. "Have you given yourself to Matashi yet?"

"What…what do you mean by that?"

A larger smile accompanied by a slight lean forward. "Have you and Mat had anal sex together, Shoju?"

"Um…no." Shoju was taken aback. "I've only ever kissed him. Why? Is that not good?"

"You tell me."

Suddenly Shoju felt as though he was treading deep waters, a feeling he didn't like. "I love kissing him, so it's good…for me." A swallow, before adding, "I suppose."

"Then it *is* good." Horo drained his cup. "But you seem rather tense."

"I'm nervous."

"Oh, I think it goes a lot deeper than that."

Shoju was once more surprised. "I don't understand, senpai."

"To clarify, to become one of the honoured of the temple, as I know it is in you to become so, you'll need to really let yourself go. Otherwise…well, you know what'll happen, don't you, Shoju?"

Shoju knew what would happen if he wasn't chosen. But that still didn't answer his question. He felt compelled to ask, "How do I do that? Let myself go, as you've suggested." Shoju's piquing curiosity eased his nerves and anxiety for a moment.

Or was it the tea he had been drinking combined with the brazier's smoke? He sure felt all warm and fuzzy inside all of a sudden, right down to the pit of his stomach.

"Show me how you touch yourself, Shoju." Master Horo poured him more tea then, again complete with all over-emphasised gestures and full of ceremony.

"I'm sorry, what?" Shoju asked incredulously as he accepted the second cup. This one was stronger. Kind of like the taste of the saké he'd had on his birthday not that long ago.

Tea didn't have alcohol in it, did it?

"Open your robe and take off your fundoshi so you can show me how you masturbate, Shoju. Then you'll truly be free once you spill your seed over yourself with me as your witness."

Shoju sat wide-eyed, frozen for a moment. "Umm..."

"Do you not understand what I've asked of you?"

"No...I do understand. I do." Shoju shifted his weight, a different anxiety now boiling within him. "It's just...I-I'm uncomfortable being naked in front of others—let alone showing others how I...pleasure myself."

"Perhaps you would like me to assist you?"

"I...beg your p-pardon?"

Master Horo stood, coming so he could sit behind Shoju, have him between his legs. "I can show you the joys of a man pleasuring another beyond a mere kiss. You'd like that, wouldn't you?"

"I'm...not s-sure."

Master Horo began untying the belt around Shoju's robe so he could open the garment. "Is it because of how you see yourself?"

Shoju gulped. "It is...I'm not lean or—"

"You are perfect."

"How can you—what?" Shoju then felt the master's hands cupping his "plump" pecs, feeling them, rubbing his heated, wanting touch all over them as his skin suddenly became sensitive there. Shoju's nipples also tingled as they became achingly erect under such erotic attention.

What a feeling!

"Mhm..." he managed as he leant into Master Horo, liking the fact he could do so; the man was a solid support behind him.

His intention, no doubt.

The master's hands kept their study of Shoju's chest, massaging them, really stimulating Shoju. He tingled all over now. He also felt himself stir, realising he would soon need his tight fundoshi removed before he did himself a mischief.

"Did you want me to assist you now?" Master Horo breathed into Shoju's ear before kissing his neck in that sensitive place that made him sigh and go weak all over.

Shoju shivered with delight. Delight he'd not felt before. Not like this. Not with someone other than Mat, anyway. "Please, t-touch me, Master Horo." His mind wandered to even greater fuzziness, now awash with carnal delights as well as the effects of the tea and smoke of the private tatami room. "Show me…how it's supposed to be done. *Please*."

"With pleasure, Shoju."

With those words, Master Horo moved his touch down Shoju's stomach, tenderly, lovingly, wantonly, before pulling away at the material of his underwear to remove it.

Now freed, Shoju's cock sprung up to greet whatever would happen next. "I'm…hard," he admitted, surprised but kind of not at the same time. After all, the atmosphere of the room, the closeness of the master, so warm, and the way he loved being touched without judgement, all contributed to that feeling.

A feeling Shoju admitted he liked.

"You have a lovely, big cock, Shoju."

"I…do?"

"Yes, you do." There were more neck kisses; he loved those most of all. "And it will be my honour to pleasure you—beginning with a special touch I know you'll appreciate."

"A s-special…touch?" Shoju heard his words but became disassociated from them while Master Horo quickly changed his intention.

"Let me show you."

Shoju nodded, the haze all around him gaining in purpose, like a miasma of delight clinging to him with an even greater success than the humidity of the mountain forests earlier.

From there, Master Horo ran his fingertips over the lip of Shoju's foreskin in little circles as it became more and more stretched over Shoju's engorging knob.

Shoju moaned.

He'd never been touched like this. So delicately and so wonderfully. But it was a touch that he realised he needed; it felt so good that it affected him to the marrow in his bones.

"Mhm…" All too soon, Shoju felt that familiar urge claw inside him, like a beast trying to escape. "You'll make me cum…quickly…" Shoju managed. "If you keep doing it…like that."

"Then cum, my handsome boy. Cum so you can let yourself go and begin the journey toward your full potential." Master Horo had now tightened his grip around Shoju's cock, tugging on it in a rhythmic motion that heightened everything even more.

Shoju soon felt the waves of his desires crash upon the shore of his needs within him.

"I'm…*oh god*…I'm cumming!" he declared as his body seemed to fold when he gave an almighty shudder and collapsed into Master Horo's embrace even more.

A shudder followed by pulse after pulse of his orgasm.

Shoju, blinded except for the sensations coursing all through him—panting, sweating, his sense of touch the only feeling available to him—felt his jizz splatter over his heated skin, right up to his chest.

Hot jizz from a hot experience, for sure.

Master Horo held Shoju in his strong arms for the longest time while he came down from his high, waiting patiently for him to cool. That time was spent giving Shoju more gentle kisses and touches of worship all over his body, from his tightened balls to his still erect nipples.

Shoju admitted he loved that.

"Your cum tastes good, Shoju. Nice and tangy, as it should be."

Shoju woke enough from his high because of those words. "It…does?" It was then he noticed his body was clean of his own fluid. When had that happened?

"And I have to tell you that you've been chosen. Congratulations."

Shoju, still too deep within the grip of his post orgasmic muddle to fully comprehend the words spoken to him, muttered, "What h-happens next?" Because he suddenly found the pleasure of succeeding, of being chosen, was nowhere near as strong as all the others within him.

Master Horo's intention, no doubt.

"You will face three trials. When you have passed them all, you'll be fully initiated into the temple as one of our honoured."

"Will I pass them all?"

"I know you will."

"When…when do I begin these trials?"

Master Horo kissed Shoju, that time on his cheek. "There is no rush, but as soon as you feel up to it. You'll need all your strength and wits about you, as they'll really test how far you can let yourself go."

"I think I understand."

"Also, you can let your mother know of your choosing, and she, like you, will be looked after for the rest of your days and given everything you both desire. More than that. That is my promise, Shoju-Kami."

Shoju found it strange to be called a god in such a way,

with the term being used as an honorific. "I'm…not a deity…"

"Oh, yes, you are. You are now the honoured, and you'll be worshipped as one by all of us from now on once you complete the trials."

Shoju was taken aback, a common theme lately. "All because I let you masturbate me?"

"It was so much more than that."

And Master Horo was right. Shoju *had* let himself go to overcome his biggest inhibition in the process. No matter how he saw himself, he was seen as something great by others. Seen as perfection.

Such a thought hit him like an epiphany.

He knew because of how others saw him, Master Horo, especially, that it was a reflection of who he truly was. It was his pure soul that had ensured he was chosen, as his mum had said right from the beginning.

Now Shoju smiled in victory.

Despite the cotton-wool feeling in his head annoying him, no doubt from the smoke and herbal tea infused with alcohol, the master clearly trying to influence him, sway his reasoning to their favour, Mat defiantly shook his head.

"I'm not doing that," he blurted with acidity. "No way."

Mat folded his arms to emphasise his stubborn but rightfully justified stance.

"You are unsure, Matashi Soju?" Master Vitus asked, offering more steaming hot tea, the aroma of which struck him hard once more.

"No." Mat declined the tea with another dismissive nod. "I'm as sure as eggs are eggs that I don't want to jerk myself off in front of you, Master Vitus. I mean no disrespect, but that sort of thing's only for my Shoju to see, not you."

A raise of a concerned eyebrow as the cup was placed down onto the tray undrunk with a clatter. "Is that your final word on the matter?"

"It is." He harrumphed through his nostrils.

A downward glance. "Then you are now an outcast, and my time here with you is done." To emphasise his words, the master got to his feet, heading for the door of the private tatami room Mat had been taken into not that long ago.

Mat was stunned, no other word for it. "You're not choosing me? For what? Not getting a hard-on and blowing my load for you to watch? This is a joke, right?"

The master turned to give Mat his last attention, still not looking him in the eyes, though. His expression was grim and tainted with disappointment and something Mat couldn't describe. "It goes deeper than that."

"What do you mean?"

A sigh. "You'll never know."

As soon as the master left the room, two temple guards entered dressed in their finest, complete with wooden plates of ceremonial armour down their fronts. "Come with us, *boy*," the biggest and meanest looking of them sneered while flexing his oiled arm muscles and cracking his knuckles one by one.

Oh, how the tone had changed; it was practically frosty now.

"Please," Mat begged after what had happened dawned on him, terribly so. "Can you go and tell Master Vitus that I would like another chance? Heck, I'll cum for him as many times as he wants me to—I'll even fill a teacup with my jizz if that's what he wants."

The two temple guards remained unmoved.

The second guard, a man no less imposing than the first, said, "Come with us or we'll drag you out by your ears. Your choice, outcast."

Mat swallowed hard.

The decision had been made.

He *was* an outcast.

Fuck!

But his thoughts suddenly weren't for himself; they were for his family. He'd failed them, like his brother before him had done so—their lives had been so difficult since that day. Failure seemed to be a family tradition.

Mat heaved a breath.

What would they do now, his family? He didn't know, other than their lives would remain hard as they tried to survive without the blessing of the temple. That, and the fact he'd never be able to see them again.

Never be able to see Shoju, either.

As he was roughly escorted out of the tatami room, tears began to fall onto his cheeks, hot and bitter. His bottom lip quivered with his grief as his heart sank into the pit of his stomach.

"I'm so sorry," was all he could say to no one, because from now on, no one would listen to him.

Mat realised he wasn't taken to the beautiful garden overlooked by the imposing wooden painted torii. No. He was hastily led toward the back of the temple's ground beyond the shadow of the honden, or main worship hall. Toward the kyozetsu, or rejection gate, as it was known. The same gate his brother had passed through before him, never to be seen again.

As soon as that gate was unlocked and opened, Mat was shoved hard in the back, no choice but for his face to find the dirt. "Oof" was all he offered as the way back inside was shut out to him with a clank of the lock being secured again.

From the other side of the imposing wall, he heard the guard laugh. Laugh his ass off, truth be told. "As the chosen begin their trials to initiate them, you, as an outcast, will endure the trials of nature if you are to survive, boy." There was then a sarcastic and vitriolic, "*Good luck!*" tacked onto his words that made Mat shiver.

More laughter, this time from the both of them, before fading away to silence.

Mat was alone.

Truly alone.

He lay in his shame for what seemed an eternity as the sun beat down to warm his back, uncomfortably so. How could the day be so beautiful when his worst nightmare had been realised?

2

A new concern found Shoju once he'd stood as instructed so he could begin his initiation trials in earnest. "Can I ask if Matashi was chosen?"

Master Horo took off Shoju's clothing, carefully folding each article before placing them down near the tea tray in a neat pile. It felt both weird and liberating to be completely naked in front of him—all except for Shoju still wearing his tabi socks, of course.

Shoju realised he didn't mind.

Master Horo replied, "Your only concern now is to let yourself be worshipped by us once you have completed what we ask of you—for you are sacred now that you've been chosen, Shoju-Kami. Don't forget that."

"Yes, Master Horo." Shoju still couldn't believe it; someone pinch him! "I'll do my best for you." He pushed his worry for Mat to the back of his thoughts…for now.

"I know you will."

Shoju had to ask. "What is the first trial I must complete?"

"Three masters will oversee each trial. The first will be

under the watchful eye of Master Fuoco, not me. I'll therefore let him explain it to you."

"Will I see you again, Master Horo?"

"You most certainly will." From a panel that'd been hidden within the wall, Master Horo produced a pure white robe made of the finest cotton, offering it to Shoju. "Let me put this on you." Master Horo did so, the robe soon tied closed by a matching belt around his waist. "But first, you will go and say goodbye to your mother. After that, return here so you can begin the first trial. Master Fuoco will be waiting for you."

"Yes, senpai."

"Please don't make Master Fuoco wait too long."

Shoju bowed, still unable to believe he'd been chosen. Him! Of all the hopeful boys this season, he was to be the honoured one—not a servant or a guard, but *the* honoured. They'd chosen him. It was a dream, one already full of delights he'd never experienced before. He was both amazed and disbelieving in equal measure. Such a strange feeling.

"I'll be as quick as I can, Master Horo."

Master Horo bowed.

The next instant, again all dream-like and wonderful, Shoju found himself in his mum's loving arms, the both of them bathed by the intense morning sun, warming them to their souls, the white of his robe glaringly bright under such intensity.

He looked like an angel. Something he knew without doubt because his mum told him so.

"You are my beautiful and handsome boy, and I'm so proud of you, Shoju. So proud. You're also my angel on

Earth because you've given both of us a great blessing. How can I ever repay you?"

Shoju felt his cheeks warm. "I honestly didn't do that much. And you don't have to do anything—you gave birth to me, looked after me, and loved me, and for that I am eternally thankful."

She dismissed him with a gentle gesture and more forehead kisses. "Whatever you did, it was more than enough. And I know you'll pass the trials to become a full member of the temple. I know it."

"I'll try."

Another forehead kiss, one full of even more love. "That's all I ask."

"I love you, Mum."

"I love you too, Shoju!"

Another embrace before Shoju tore himself away from her, feeling the urgency of the situation overwhelm him all of a sudden. He wanted to get on with things.

"I'll see you soon, Mum. Bye!"

The pleasant walk to the tatami room where he'd become the chosen was unlike any walk he'd done before in his life. It was full of hope and acceptance and trust in both himself and the masters that whatever happened next, it was they who wanted him to succeed.

And that was a very different feeling to experience—so strange but so wonderful at the same time, having someone else believing in him. Wow! And not just one person, but six. The six Masters of the temple, too. Shoju couldn't help but become a little overwhelmed as he entered the fragrant and smoky tatami room once more.

As soon as he'd done so, and as if by magic—or great timing—Master Fuoco appeared like an apparition through the haze. Shoju gasped. The man was holding a few bundles of rope made of what Shoju believed was jute, evident from the shiny fibres within its construction.

He became instantly curious, but let Master Horo explain.

"The first trial is the Trial of Endurance, Shoju-Kami." Master Fuoco stepped forward, smiling. "Have you heard of the art of shibari before?"

Shoju had to admit he hadn't. "No, senpai, I haven't."

"Then this will be an interesting experience for you," Master Fuoco replied. "One that will test you in the most artful way, I know it."

Shoju bowed. "Yes, senpai."

"Please take off your robe." The man began undoing one of the bundles of rope. "I need you to be naked for your first trial, Shoju-Kami."

At that, Shoju paused, his stomach tightening. "Um, did I hear you say you want me...want me to be *naked*, Master Fuoco?"

Master Fuoco looked up, eyes glinting. "I heard from Master Horo that you are most pleasing to witness in your natural state and that you've been blessed with the full bounty of the gods between your legs, too. Therefore, I know you are beautiful, as that is what Master Horo speaks, and he always tells the truth."

"The truth is, I don't see myself like that. As being beautiful, I mean."

Master Fuoco smiled. "That is why we have shibari as

the first trial. Being tied up and admired, worshipped, and brought to climax while under someone else's complete control will help you realise this as you become an even more wondrous work of art."

Something struck Shoju the most out of all that, and he had to ask, "You…I need to ejaculate again?"

"Yes. As you will need to do so for each of the trials today."

Shoju became overwhelmed. "I've only ever come twice in a day at the most before; I don't usually like touching myself. And I certainly don't know if I can do it *that* many times, honest." He then hung his head. "I don't want to disappoint you or any of the other masters, Master Horo most of all."

Master Fuoco came closer. "With all of us helping you, I have no doubt you'll never disappoint us. We believe in you, Shoju-Kami; that's why you were chosen."

"I'll do my best."

"Good." Master Fuoco bowed slightly. "Now, please disrobe so we can begin."

"Yes, senpai." With a newfound confidence, the scents of the tatami room overwhelming him again, making him light-headed once more, Shoju slipped off his robe. As soon as the material fell to his ankles, he could see he had a proud semi already.

Master Fuoco took in a delighted breath. "You are wondrous. Truly wondrous. How can you not see yourself as such?"

"I'm too fat, and I'm—"

"Don't talk like that. You are so beautiful in my eyes it

almost blinds me." Master Fuoco gently grabbed Shoju's cock, rubbing his thumb over the top of his knob where his foreskin still covered it, sending little delightful shivers all through him.

Shoju moaned. "Then I believe I'm ready for my trial, Master Fuoco."

"Before we begin, I must establish your comfort levels."

Shoju had no idea what the man spoke of, but before he could ask there were more words added, "What might it sound like if you're in distress?" the man asked gently. "And what might it sound like if you're doing okay, Shoju?"

"I'm...not sure."

"At the foundation of every experience, there needs to be trust," Fuoco offered. "Do you trust me?"

"I do, senpai."

Master Fuoco continued to run his gentle attention over Shoju's engorging cock. "I already know the sounds of your pleasure."

"Mhm, yes!" Shoju replied, feeling giddy all of a sudden.

But before he could get into the groove of being pleasured, become swept away by the moment as he'd done when Master Horo masturbated him, Master Fuoco squeezed Shoju's now fully swollen cock head so that pain shot through him, right to his stomach and balls. "Ah!" he shouted, short and sharp and with a hiss between his teeth at the end of it.

"And now I know what you sound like when you don't like something."

Eyes watery, Shoju replied, "You sure do."

"Good." He was pleasured again before Master Fuoco let go. "We can begin."

"What do you want me to do, senpai?"

Master Fuoco went behind Shoju. "Put your hands behind your back and grab hold of your elbows; I'll bind them first."

Shoju did so without delay, wanting to get on with things. Because despite the shock of Master Fuoco's harsh grip earlier, startling him more than anything, he hadn't softened.

In fact, his cock was as hard as ever.

And as Shoju felt the rope being tied around his hands and arms, pulled tight and knotted to set it in place so he couldn't move, Master Fuoco said, "I see that you're leaking pre-cum now, Shoju-Kami. Does it excite you, knowing that I'll soon have you at my mercy? That I'll soon be able to do as I please to you to get you to cum for me?"

"Yes," Shoju admitted with a swallow. "Yes, it does, senpai."

"Excellent."

Master Fuoco soon stood in front of Shoju. He pulled the length of rope around Shoju's chest to bind it as much as his hands and arms were behind him. It was also pulled tightly, the compression already an odd sensation, but certainly not uncomfortable. In fact, Shoju found he was comforted by the closeness of everything against his skin.

"Tie me up so I can't move at all, senpai." Shoju felt his cock pulse with his growing anticipation and leak more, too. "I want to be at your mercy!"

"And you will be, I promise." Master Fuoco placed his

hand on Shoju's shoulder. "Now, lie down so I can bind your legs."

"What will you do to me then?"

"I'll show you the sensual and unique delights of my mouth against your hardness as I suck the cum from out of your ripened balls, Shoju-Kami. That's what I'll do to you."

"Oh…my, yes!" Shoju went all funny inside after hearing that, wonderfully so.

He also couldn't help but let out a giggle, one that made Master Fuoco smile. As such, Shoju quickly did as he was asked, lying on the tatami matting without delay. He licked his lips, saliva dripping, while he patiently waited for Master Fuoco to bind his legs, the man making sure he was in the perfect position for the greatest effectiveness.

Shoju remained as hard as ever.

And while the master worked studiously and with ceremony, Shoju thought about how he'd never been given a blowjob before. And sure, even though he would have wanted Mat to be his first, Master Fuoco's mouth would be just as wonderful. He knew this because there was no doubt the man worshipped him; his touch, his attention, and his care were all evidence of that.

"I'm all yours, senpai," he muttered, feeling overwhelmed and doing his best to try and not orgasm too soon. "Make me cum now you've bound me."

"You are all of ours, Shoju-Kami. And it will be my pleasure to bring you to your climax," Master Fuoco declared when the tying was done.

Shoju tried to squirm, unable to do so thanks to the rope, artfully knotted, beautifully so, too, which immobilised him. He had to admit, he liked the feeling of being so helpless under the attention of such a strong, determined man.

"Suck my dick, senpai. Let me give you your reward for what you've done for me, for I do feel beautiful now that I'm like this before you."

"That's the spirit!" And with that, Master Fuoco moved so his lips could kiss Shoju's painfully engorged knob, all wet with his excitement. "You taste so good, too. So good."

Again, Shoju tried to move, shivers of delight trembling all through him, making him arch his back and hiss through his teeth. "I won't last long."

"I told you having another help you would mean you could orgasm many times in a row, didn't I?"

"You did."

"Then let's not delay. Master Vitus is waiting to begin the second trial with you."

Before Shoju could answer, the kisses all over his sensitive places soon engulfed him as Master Fuoco took his cock fully into his mouth, so warm and wet and wonderful. Shoju let out a moan, one that reflected the carnal delights that swirled within him, needing to be let out.

Shoju came.

He also shuddered, unable to control himself. "Yes!" he called out as the biting of the rope enhanced the delivery into the man's mouth with an even greater intensity than he'd ever felt before.

He came and came, stomach quivering and legs shaking as he did so. It was then he felt something different. The pain of suddenly not being able to move properly while he fell into his body's mercy was something so profound that he became blinded by it. He sucked in great heaves of air as best he could, considering his chest was bound and breathing in deeply was limited.

What he managed, the intake he accomplished under such restraint, fuelled the remaining pulses of his orgasm. The rush of it was unbelievable. To be so weak yet so powerful at the same time was an incredible feeling.

Shoju moaned and moaned, saliva dripping even more, as he gave everything he had to his master. The blowjob he'd received drained every drop from him in a way unlike any other. He was unable to quantify the experience, it was that wonderful and strange all in one.

He moaned even more.

When he was finally spent, exhausted to his bones and drenched with sweat, the man moved to comfort him, even if he didn't untie the ropes.

Perhaps Master Fuoco wasn't finished with him yet.

No matter, because as Shoju cooled, he was pulled across the tatami matting so he could be held lovingly. "You *are* perfect, Shoju-Kami. Perfect."

But Shoju, now calming from his climatic high, began to feel too restrained by the ropes. "When will you untie me, now that I've given you what you asked for?"

"Patience." A kiss upon Shoju's lips, warm and salty with his own tang. "Master Vitus requires you remain within the grip of the shibari for the next trial."

"What will that be?"

"I'll let him tell you. For now, let me comfort you and give you all of my attention, for you deserve nothing less."

"Yes, senpai."

The kiss from Master Fuoco deepened then, and Shoju couldn't help but become lost within it as their saliva-dripping tongues danced the dance of delight within each other's mouths.

Shoju could get used to this.

Mat didn't move for ages.

He couldn't.

What was the point?

He was as good as dead, anyway. He might as well lie here and let himself rot into the ground. That was all he was useful for now, his decomposing body nothing but fertiliser for the next generation of straw flowers that popped up in the springtime here and there wherever light filtered down from the canopy.

He felt so desperately alone.

So utterly and completely defeated, too.

Mat was a failure. And as that thought sunk in deeper, right down to the darkest part of him, spreading all through him like a cancer, he began to cry—big, heaving drops of his grief.

Grief not only for himself, but for a family he'd never see again. For Shoju too. His sweet and beautiful

companion, who he wished he could hold one last time. Tell him that he loved him again.

"Are you going to get up?" a stranger's voice lilted. "Or have you already resigned yourself to the fact you've been defeated by those assholes, huh?"

Mat, unable to fathom how there could be anyone else out here with him, looked up in disbelief through his watery eyes. Wiping them, he then took in a sharp intake of breath as his gaze fell upon one of the most handsome men he'd ever seen—aside from Shoju, of course.

He was tall, dark-haired, and soft-faced, but strangely he had sparkling blue-eyes that seemed to glint whenever the dappling light fell on him just so. That colour was very rare. Mat hadn't seen anyone with eyes like that before.

He was intrigued.

The man also had a presence about him Mat couldn't describe, foreboding but not in any dominating way. A presence that seemed to kick up things within him Mat had never expected, like a summer's breeze came and swept away the cobwebs around the eaves of his home.

He felt weird within the man's shadow, that's for sure.

"Who…are you?" he found himself blurting while he continued to examine the stranger…no, while he became fascinated by him.

"My name is Akai—and who might you be, the one they now call outcast?"

"My name's Matashi. Matashi Soju." Mat got up onto his knees. "Why are you…how are you here?"

A snort of laughter from Akai as he offered his hand.

"One of us always waits at the rejection gate on this day every selection season. This year it's my turn."

As soon as Mat grabbed Akai's hand so he could be helped to his feet, another strange feeling overcame him, one unlike any other. A feeling that jolted right through him to settle within his balls and make his cock stir, no lie. He'd never felt such a thing before.

What the hell was that about?

He quickly pulled away his hand, unsure. "What…what was that?"

A questioning look. "What was what?"

"The…weird sensation that went all through me when I touched you."

"Oh, *that*." A knowing smile formed on Akai's full lips, complete with an eyebrow raise. "That's just my emerging heat you're sensing. I'm coming to my first cycle—which is why I was chosen to be here now, I might add."

"Your what?"

Akai then looked around, suddenly seeming nervous. "I'll tell you everything you need to know very soon, Matashi. But for the here and now, we *must* get away from the wall. If the temple's guards see me, they'll kill me without so much as a second thought."

"Why would they do that?" Mat got up to stand next to Akai, feeling weakened from the grief still swirling inside him. Another touch by Akai, this time on Mat's shoulder. As soon as the connection was made, the same weird feeling spread from that contact to settle where it did before, causing him to get hard, achingly so.

Mat tried to ignore it.

"Because, and to put it simply for now, I'm the enemy, that's why." With that, Akai gestured for Mat to follow him. "So, let's go before something far more terrible happens than you being kicked out of a sanctioned sex cult with an agenda."

Mat became confused. "A what?"

Akai didn't answer, now charging ahead to disappear within the thick trees beyond the temple's walls. Mat, having no choice, followed Akai into the depths of the forest.

But as he gingerly stepped through the thick undergrowth, trying to keep up with the man who'd rescued him, he wished he had worn more practical clothing and shoes than the ceremonial ones he was now burdened with.

When another man entered the private tatami room, Shoju didn't know. What with the deep and loving kisses he'd received and reciprocated from Master Fuoco, the intoxicating smoke all around him, and the arousing feeling of still being at the man's mercy thanks to remaining bound by the ropes, Shoju was lost within himself.

So lost, it was wonderful.

A shadow fell over Shoju. Moments later, he felt a warm and gentle hand cup his balls after Master Fuoco spread his legs, no doubt in preparation for his next trial—

one that had already begun now that he realised there was another in the room with him.

He craned his neck to gaze upon who he assumed was Master Vitus, a man with long dark hair tied in a ribbon, deep soulful eyes, and a deeper expression. He looked to be a serious man, Shoju believed. But despite that, he had a pleasant demeanour, made more so by the careful way he moved, practiced and methodical.

By the way he touched Shoju, too.

The man was old, older than Master Fuoco, that's for sure. Master Vitus curled his lips with not only lust, but what Shoju had begun to understand was admiration.

Admiration for him.

To confirm those thoughts, Master Vitus said, "What the others have said about you is true, Shoju-Kami. You *are* perfection personified. A truly beautiful boy. Truly beautiful."

Shoju smiled, loving the intention of the man's words. The compliment as well. "Thank you, senpai."

"And I'll so enjoy worshipping you while I guide you through the second trial, that much I know." To Master Fuoco, he nodded. "Ready?"

"Ready," Master Fuoco replied, not making any move to get up.

"Will you be staying here for this trial, Master Fuoco?" Shoju asked curiously.

"I will be, yes."

Shoju smiled, looking up affectionately at the man who still held him, who'd been kissing him so wonderfully that his lips tingled and who had a warmth within Shoju welcomed. "Then I'm ready."

Master Vitus said, "Please get Shoju-Kami into position for me, Master Fuoco. I'll then introduce him to the delights of erotic cupping and body fluid worship as we begin the next trial: the Trial of Tolerance."

Shoju asked, "Um...what's erotic cupping?"

"It's best if we show you," Master Fuoco replied, brushing his hand tenderly over Shoju's cheek. "But understand, Master Vitus and I will be gentle and go slowly with you. We both want to make sure you're prepared properly for everything that follows as well, including the final trial with Master Ito."

"Thank you, senpai," Shoju said to him. "I appreciate that."

"Good boy," Master Vitus chimed in, reaching to open an ornately carved wooden case full of bulbous glass cups Shoju only then noticed was next to the man. "We shall begin, then."

If Shoju thought Master Fuoco's engulfing kisses were something to crave for, he quickly found out that was nothing after he was placed into position on his back upon the tatami matting so the two men could be on either side of him.

It began with the skin of his chest not covered by the rope—including his nipples, still sensitive from his recent orgasm—being oiled by Master Vitus' careful attention. Once they were rubbed and teased, coming hard to the point of aching because of it, Shoju, unable to help himself, moaned and arched his back, his tongue lolling out of his open mouth, salivating. He loved this. The man then concentrated on even more sensitive places, from his neck to the area between his anus and balls.

"So pretty," Master Vitus said as he prepared the next step of the proceedings, getting the cups ready.

While this happened, Master Fuoco continued to knead the oil into Shoju's skin. At the same time, he lowered himself so his lips came tantalisingly close to Shoju's without making contact. He could feel the man's warm breath caress him where it mattered.

Shoju moaned again, more desperate that time.

"Open your mouth wider for me, Shoju-Kami," Master Fuoco asked.

Shoju did so without delay.

And as Shoju felt the warm glass of the cups being pressed against him, moments later accompanied by a sharp pinch that stung before dissipating as they attached, Master Fuoco dribbled a thick drool of his saliva into Shoju's waiting mouth.

"It has begun," Master Vitus declared as he applied more and more cups all over Shoju's chest, stomach, and the place just above his pubic hair.

It kind of felt weird having his skin pulled in such a way. It wasn't distressing, though. Far from it. But what surprised Shoju the most, aside from the pleasant but mildly tangy taste of Master Fuoco's saliva washing all over his tongue, was that the cups that'd been placed on his nipples gave him wonderfully delightful chills of ecstasy all through him.

To be honest, Shoju almost became overwhelmed by

everything happening to him, including once more harbouring a proud erection Master Vitus liked to caress often. Although Shoju noticed the man liked to play with his foreskin most of all.

He didn't mind that.

Master Fuoco spat into Shoju's mouth again. "Don't swallow," he ordered as he did so.

Shoju nodded his head in understanding.

With the cupping completed as far as Shoju could tell, Master Vitus added his saliva to Master Fuoco's in his mouth, both men taking turns to dribble their spittle onto Shoju's tongue.

Shoju's mouth was soon full.

But what happened next surprised him most of all. Both masters took turns kissing him deeply, tongues dancing, their kisses now lubricated with all the saliva they'd given Shoju, including his own because he'd had his mouth open so long.

What a way to share such passionate kisses, ones that were wet, sloppy, and sucking, yet intoxicatingly arousing. Shoju moaned and moaned, writhing as best as he was able, considering he was bound by the rope that now seemed to bite into him as much as the cups upon his heated skin.

But, by god, he was awakened again. Aching now, especially his hard cock, which was leaking his excitement even more than before. How was such a thing possible? But there it was. Incredible.

Shoju hadn't felt like this, ever! So worshipped and admired, it overwhelmed him, truly. He trembled; he really did. He also considered himself lucky, and felt sorry for those who weren't chosen, or were to be the guards or the servants of the temple.

Not the honoured, like him.

By the time Shoju was light-headed and numb all over because of all the attention he'd received—all those kisses too—Master Fuoco sat up, wiping his mouth of his efforts.

Master Vitus said, "You may swallow now, Shoju-Kami."

Shoju did so, enjoying the feeling and the thought of a part of them being taken down inside him as he felt their saliva slide down his throat.

"You'll now take our cum into your mouth," Master Fuoco announced. "We'll then milk you of yours to add that into your mouth too. From there, we will share kisses again, but ones that'll be lubricated by the fluids of our love for you instead."

Shoju shuddered. He liked the sound of that. "Give me all of your cum. I want to taste it. I need it."

"Good boy," Master Vitus said as he too sat up, quickly freeing his cock from his fundoshi, a thick veiny beauty that had a huge knob as shiny and ripe as a new season's apple.

Master Fuoco did the same—his not as big but no less impressive.

Shoju noted how both men were circumcised.

But before he could think of a reason why, before he could even blink, really, they both began masturbating themselves, coming closer so Shoju could smell their manly muskiness.

An intoxicating scent, indeed.

"You're so perfect," Master Vitus moaned as his

motions upon himself intensified. "I can't wait to cum so I can see my jizz cover your lips and go into your mouth."

"Give it to me," Shoju encouraged as he began to feel the effects of such closeness. He was the object of their desires, restrained and cupped for their added pleasure, and surprised he was able to tolerate it, too.

He knew it was because he *was* theirs, not wanting it any other way.

"You will be even prettier with our cum covering your face," Master Fuoco said with the groans of his approaching climax—Shoju could tell he was close.

Shoju was close, too.

Then it happened. Both men, groaning, feverishly moving their hands over themselves, faster and faster, quivering, almost simultaneously ejaculated thick, hot ribbons of their jizz into Shoju's open and eager mouth.

As he knew it would, a lot of it missed its mark. Sure, most went where he wanted it, tasting the salty tang immediately, but a lot went all over his lips and cheeks. Some even made it to his eyebrow.

But that didn't matter.

Both men, flushed and sweating from their efforts, began licking and kissing their cum off Shoju's face with affection, tenderness, and moans of delight, ensuring any accompanying kisses were flavoured by their ejaculate.

Shoju loved it.

But he knew he was now quickly approaching the point of no return. As such, between their affection, the air heated and electric between them, Shoju managed, "I w-won't... last l-long."

Master Vitus didn't waste any time.

Neither did Master Fuoco.

Both men were paying attention to Shoju's erection with their mouths. To have two men give him a blowjob, that sure was something. With an almighty shudder, one that grew from every fibre of his being, he soon felt that all too familiar rush within him.

He began panting.

Aching.

Gasping.

"I'm…going to cum!" Shoju shouted, unable to move but not caring either as he delivered his load into two wanting mouths.

After that, exhausted, sweating, and completely drained right down to his balls, he was once more kissed and kissed. That time, his own flavour was added to the passion.

Shoju didn't know how long they did that to him, but when he had cooled enough, he was quickly untied, and the cups were removed.

He felt such relief.

Wow!

Master Fuoco held Shoju for another age, caressing, kissing, and comforting him. Shoju never wanted to be out of the man's arms, not ever.

But he knew this moment wouldn't last forever.

"I must leave you now," Master Fuoco said to confirm Shoju's thoughts. "But I'll return, I promise."

Shoju couldn't speak, still so affected, but he nodded his understanding. His balls ached terribly because he'd ejaculated three times already in as many hours. They'd be sore for ages, he knew. What he didn't know was whether or not he could cum again so soon for the last trial.

He hoped he could.

Now left alone, Shoju took the time to gather himself, to meditate, in a way. He closed his eyes, thanking his lucky stars for his fortune. What else could he do? He had to wait. That's what was expected of him, so that's what he would do.

He was their good boy.

"Do you believe he'll be worthy?" Shoju thought he heard Master Fuoco say in the haze and confusion of his post-orgasmic state from beyond the door of the tatami room.

"He will be perfect," was the reply; from whom Shoju wasn't sure.

Another voice—one he believed was Master Vitus—said, "Then we'll have to make sure we have him prepared properly before the next choosing season is upon us."

"Agreed," the unrecognisable voice said. "Let the others know of our decision. That is the way of the temple."

"Yes, Master Ito."

Shoju couldn't grasp the rest of what was said, as there was more. Mostly because, even though he was now free to move around, no sooner did he try to concentrate, he couldn't. Not only was so much loving attention affecting him, he believed the smoke was too. What *were* they burning in that little brazier? Something intoxicating, no doubt. A special kind of herb, maybe?

But he didn't have time to contemplate such matters.

Another man entered the room, one distinguished and a lot older than the other Masters, even Master Vitus. "My name is Master Ito, Shoju-Kami. And I'm here to help you get through your final trial."

"Yes, senpai," Shoju replied while he got up onto his elbows, shaking and still feeling weak.

"But first, if you can, I want you to get up onto your knees. I need to know how good you are at sucking my cock."

Shoju was taken aback. "I...don't understand."

Master Ito opened his robe, an action that revealed his bulge within his fundoshi all too well. "A boy must not only be appreciative when he receives pleasure, but he must also learn to give it with just as much grace as well. That is the way of the temple. That is also your way now. Do you understand, Shoju-Kami?"

"I do." Shoju got up as ordered, slowly, even though the weakness from his earlier rush didn't dissipate as quickly as he'd have liked. He swallowed. "And I'll do my best to please you."

"I know you will." The man beamed a smile. "Now come free my cock so you can pleasure it with your mouth—I'll instruct you as needed. Teach you how to do it properly, if you will."

"Yes, sensei."

Master Ito smiled at the change in Shoju's honorific.

3

Mat followed Akai as best he could for bloody ages through thick undergrowth that caught and snagged his robe, forested gullies where he fell many times—cuts and scratches all over him—and open clearings where refreshing pools glistened under the intense summer sun, most of them he fell onto his knees before to drink his fill, feeling exhausted.

"We have a long way to go, Matashi." Akai glanced around, worry on his brow as Mat quenched his thirst at the latest pool as best he could. "A *long* way to go before we're safe."

Mat groaned disapprovingly. "Just let me lie down so I can die here on this shore in peace, please."

Akai offered his hand. "Did you want me to help you?"

Mat sat up. "No!" he snapped, his stomach getting that fluttery feeling inside—the feeling he got whenever he thought of being intimate with Shoju.

At that thought, sadness stabbed at him.

He'd never see Shoju again.

Akai looked at him, puzzlement rising above his concern. "What's wrong?"

"Nothing." Mat swallowed. "It's just that…well, I've only just gotten rid of the boner you gave me when you touched me the first time."

Akai laughed lightly, placing his hands on his hips. "You're my Alpha, Matashi; that's why you stir inside like you do when I touch you. No one else would be affected like that. Only you. But it's nothing to worry about if you go with it, trust me."

Mat *did* trust Akai…and that was a funny thing, too. He didn't even know the man. But there it was. His trust. "This has to do with that heat thing you talked about earlier, right?"

"Correct."

"I'm trying, but I really don't understand."

"That's because I haven't explained everything to you yet. Don't worry, when we get to my home within the secret village, I'll tell you everything."

"Um…what if I don't…'go with it,' as you say? I mean, only an hour or so ago, I thought I was going to be with Shoju for the rest of my life because he was my named companion. Now…now I don't know what the heck's going on."

"I'll explain everything soon, but we must go. The temple's guards patrol around here often. If they catch us, we'll be killed on sight. You can trust me on that, as well."

Mat sighed. "I've got no choice, have I?"

"Don't talk like that."

"I can't help it." Mat managed a smile, also feeling at ease in Akai's presence. "It's my defeatist personality shining through that drives my cynicism."

"Ah, noted."

They both laughed.

Mat, looking up at Akai, right into those amazing blues, asked, "I'm not going to see Shoju ever again, am I?"

"If he was chosen, whether for a guard, a servant, or the honoured, no. No, you're not. The Cult of Men keep the boys they select to themselves, conveniently getting rid of those who stand in their way."

"Now *that* I can understand." And it was true. Mat had already experienced the cold, hard reality of being an outcast. He hated to imagine what would happen to those who also defied the temple.

He shuddered at that thought.

Akai offered his hand again. "Let's go, Matashi. *Please.*"

Mat nodded, a gesture he knew meant he'd resigned himself to the fact he did need help. Needed it badly. He knew he was in no condition to venture unassisted through the wilds, being a stablehand in his previous life.

He got to his feet with Akai's assistance, already sore all over from his awkward sprint through the forest. He felt like an old man, if he was being honest. And yep, as expected, the electricity of their contact shot straight through him to stiffen his cock, causing it to ache being so restrained within the cloth of his fundoshi.

This was going to be an interesting journey. One made even more so because his shoes had broken god knows when; as such, he now trod the uneven forest floor in nothing but his tabi socks. Not a good thing, really. Many times, a twig or stone seemed to stab at the soles of his feet, causing him to yelp.

He did a lot of yelping.

And it was both a saviour and a hindrance how Akai kept holding Mat's hand as they made their way toward his village. Yes, he was saved from a nastier fall many times, but at the same time…well, how long could he have a hard-on without needing relief?

Not long, Mat imagined.

"I reckon I'm gonna get blue balls for days," Mat said after another hour or so of trudging through the forest harbouring an impressive erection, one that didn't ease, not one inch. "All because of you and what you're doing to me, you know."

Akai smiled. "I know the cure for that."

"I bet you do." But Mat managed a smile again.

Akai winked. "I know many different methods when it comes to pleasuring my Alpha; I've been training for it for my whole life."

"Really?" Mat realised this was serious for Akai.

Akai explained, "Once an Alpha and Omega have bonded, then it's for life. How could I not be prepared for that?"

"And…seeing as I'm supposed to be your—"

"Yes, we're bonded," Akai interjected. "As I know that was your question. I could see it forming in your eyes simply by the way you looked at me, both unsure and curious at the same time. It's quite endearing, really."

"I…see." Mat swallowed hard, feeling his cheeks warm.

"The first time I touched you, it happened—our bonding."

"But what if I don't want to be bonded to you?"

Akai took a deep breath at Mat's question. "The further I get into my first heat over the course of the next month, the more the urges within the both of us will increase until they overtake us. The only relief from that will be when we consummate our bond. Therefore, I promise you, what you want now will not be what you want by the time the next moon waxes to its fullest. Again, you can trust me on that."

"I don't even know you," Mat said, stating the bleeding obvious as far as he was concerned. "Because if I'm getting this right, I've got to fuck you to stop this feeling I get whenever you touch me, right?"

"Yes, you must mate with me."

Mat was taken aback. To hear it confirmed rather than suspect it shook him to his core. "Let's just get to this village of yours first. We can talk later about all this, okay?"

"As you wish, my Alpha." Akai pulled his hand away, letting Mat go. "It's just over that rise and beyond the waterfall gate."

"Then let's go." Mat missed Akai's hold. "And don't call me your Alpha. I'm Matashi. Simply Matashi. All right?"

Akai bowed his head. "Of course…Matashi."

Mat then found himself saying the most bizarre thing. "Even though you're not Shoju…I think you're very handsome."

"I think you're the most beautiful man I've ever seen."

Mat snorted. "You would say that."

"For someone who's going to give me their baby as soon as we've mated, what else *could* I say?"

Mat was stunned and stood frozen. "Wait! What?"

Shoju tugged down the material of Master Ito's fundoshi eagerly, freeing the man's stiffened cock as instructed. It wasn't as big as Master Fuoco's, or even Master Vitus' either, but it did have one thing in common with them.

"You're circumcised…like Master Vitus and Master Fuoco are," Shoju blurted, unable to help himself. Mat and his other friends he'd seen in the public baths—when he felt brave enough to attend them—were uncut as he was, so this was the first time seeing cut ones.

Not that it mattered.

Dick was dick.

Master Ito nodded. "To become a temple master, that part must be given to the Kami who live within the sacred walls here to protect us. That is the way of the temple."

Shoju couldn't help but feel a little uncomfortable at that notion. Having it done as an adult, it'd hurt like hell. Wouldn't it? "If I became a temple master, I'd have to have that done to me then, right?"

"You'll always be the honoured, Shoju-Kami, never a master."

Shoju found relief in those words. "I'm glad of it."

"So am I." The man placed his hands upon Shoju's head, pulling him closer to his throbbing, leaking cock, so much so Shoju's lips just touched it. He could taste the salt of the man's arousal already. The tangy bitterness of it, too.

"Now show me how you use your mouth, boy. But take it slowly to make sure you give me your full attention."

"Yes, sensei."

Although, before he got down to the business in earnest, Shoju had to use his hand around the root of Master's Ito's cock to pull it into a better position for easier access. The man's obvious arousal, his twitching hardness, now leaking a thread of clear fluid, meant it was completely vertical, almost touching his stomach. Not easy to get to at all, considering Shoju was on his knees and looking up at the tall man.

But get there, he did.

"Hmm, that's it," Master Ito said, holding Shoju's head with more intent. "Do what you need to do so you can pleasure me properly. I like when you do."

Shoju, at first hesitant under such scrutiny, anxious as usual and licking his lips because of it, soon took as much of Master Ito's cock into his mouth as he dared. He didn't want to rush. He wanted to enjoy the experience, too. He also made sure he used plenty of saliva for his action, lubricating everything nicely, as he knew was the right and proper thing to do. And even though Master Ito's cock wasn't large, as he'd noted when he first saw it, the thing was certainly a mouthful, nevertheless.

With each passing moment, he tried to take it in as deeply as he could manage. In no time at all, Shoju soon found having it touch the back of his tongue something that not only felt uncomfortable, but made him recoil as well.

He spluttered as he pulled away.

"Don't try and deep-throat it too soon—that requires

training to be able to do properly. I told you to take it slowly, boy. Do as you've been told, please."

Shoju, saliva dripping onto his chest from his lips and chin, the cup and rope marks still evident there, coughed a few times in recovery from his over eagerness. "I u-understand that…now, sensei."

"First, concentrate your attention on the head of my cock. Use your tongue and apply enough suction to please me."

"May I ask how much suction is needed to please you the best?"

He gave a smile, one lust-filled and wide. "Imagine you're trying to suck up a thick drink through a straw. That would be sufficient."

"Yes, sensei."

Shoju did as asked, soon finding he was getting into a rhythm. He even began enjoying it, finally. Mostly because the feeling of being connected to another man in such a way sure was special to him. It was different, too. What made it even better were the moans of delight and the man's strong fingers massaging the top of his head to indicate his approval.

That couldn't be beat.

With his saliva dribbling off his chin even more, Shoju sucked, slurped, and gave his all as he pleasured Master Ito the best he could. All the while, and without even realising it, the man was pushing Shoju to go deeper and deeper as he became used to things.

Shoju continued eagerly.

Until, and with his nose deep in Master Ito's thick

black pubes, he began to feel giddy, no longer able to breathe properly through his flared nostrils while he serviced the man, while he tried to work him up to orgasm to get his reward for his efforts.

"You make me so hard, boy," Master Ito announced. "But let's see how much you can take now you've become accustomed to what's required of you, hmm?"

Shoju, affected by the limited air getting to him—seeing as his mouth was stuffed with cock to the back of his throat, eyes watering, almost gagging as a result—could only groan in response.

Mater Ito must have taken that as a signal to pull at Shoju's head even more, holding him even tighter to ensure he couldn't move away even if he wanted to. "Take it for as long as you can."

Another groan.

Shoju could feel the air get thin, his extremities go numb; his vision became blurry. He was beyond gagging, because now he could only think about taking a breath. A life-saving, wonderful breath.

But Master Ito didn't let him go.

"Take it deeper, boy. Do your best for me, as you said you would."

Shoju began to shake, his legs most of all; his lungs felt as though they would burst, needing air, sweet, sweet air. His mind became a complete muddle as Master Ito began to thrust while holding onto Shoju for dear life, it seemed. Shoju groaned and groaned. He also began gagging and spluttering now, unable to pull away.

At the point where he thought he would faint from the

lack of oxygen, that's when the man let him go. Shoju fell into a heap on the matting, heaving in great breaths.

Such relief.

He'd completely collapsed, unable to do anything else but shake, cough, and gasp for breath. His body was useless for anything else. He heaved and heaved, too, unsure if he was going to vomit or not.

Shoju didn't like this bit.

He felt so weak, so vulnerable. But there was also another feeling there as well. One he couldn't quantify…not at first.

What had happened?

He wiped his mouth of what he thought was his saliva because he was drenched in his own drool, so why wouldn't he think that? But no, what he thought were his own efforts were far from it.

He wiped Master Ito's thick cum from off his chin.

It was then he knew the feeling.

The feeling of accomplishment.

"I m-made…you cum," Shoju said through his muddled mind, his voice hoarse as the tangy and very salty reward washed through his mouth.

"You pleased me greatly, Shoju-Kami. And you did so with grace, as is the way of the temple. For that, I'll be more than happy to help you through the next trial."

"What's…the next trial…to b-be?" Shoju tried to get up, but for a moment was still held in place by his failings. His weak body was made even weaker because of the deprivation he'd just endured.

Master Ito stepped closer, grabbing Shoju to place him

on all fours without ceremony. "Lower your head and raise your buttocks, boy. The next trial is known as the Trial of Preparation. For it, I'll introduce you to the pleasure of anal stimulation and prostate play. Do you understand?"

"I...do."

"Good. Then let us begin." A moment followed where Shoju couldn't see Master Ito, before the man added, "But be warned, an orgasm created in such a way will leave you incapacitated for a while. It's one of the deepest and most profound climaxes you'll ever experience, and it will be my pleasure to give you your first taste of it. So please, relax and let me take control of your body while I worship you."

Shoju said, "That is the t-temple way, right?"

"It is."

Master Ito moved Shoju's legs wider apart as he began caressing him all over, concentrating on his buttocks, of course. Shoju all of a sudden felt vulnerable, more so than before, the intent of the position he was placed into, no doubt.

"You have magnificent balls, boy," Master Ito complimented as they were cupped and fondled.

"Thank you, sensei."

"But the most magnificent part of you is your anus. It's a true beauty, puckered and pink and begging for me to pleasure it. And pleasure it, I will. Are you ready?"

"I am, sensei."

Shoju heard a bottle being uncapped, followed by the sound of what he only assumed was some sort of lubricant or oil being poured into the man's hands. A moment later, and with a pleasant sensation that sent a jolt through him to settle at the base of his spine, Master Ito rubbed his slicked fingers over the part of Shoju that he wanted to worship.

"Feels good, doesn't it, boy?"

Shoju was surprised by how nice it did feel. "It does."

"Then be prepared for penetration, as that is how I will truly show you what it's like to be pleasured."

"Yes, sensei."

True to his word, and after a little more preparation that made Shoju's lips quiver and his legs turn to jelly below his knees, Master Ito's finger was gently pushed inside Shoju.

Shit!

Shoju sucked in a sharp breath as a stab of pain resulted, one that coursed all through him but seemed to burn the most at the point where he was entered.

Master Ito asked, "Are you all right, Shoju-Kami?"

Shoju needed a moment, noting how the man didn't remove his finger but at the same time didn't move it either. "Give…give me a m-minute, please."

"As you wish."

Shoju knew he had to relax. He tried to breathe more evenly, eventually doing so as Master Ito's touch remained within him. "I'm ready."

"You are very tight, boy."

"I'm sorry."

"Don't be—you'll just need to be trained so you don't experience so much pain when you're worshipped in this way."

"Then train me please, sensei."

As the man moved his finger inside Shoju once more, finding that exquisite place quickly, an action that sent tingles and a strange but warm sensation all through him, right to the deepest part of him, he said, "That's my intention. As such, Shoju-Kami, I want you to try and remain as relaxed as you can for me. Keep breathing, too."

Shoju nodded. "I'll do my best." But saying such a thing and doing it were two completely different things, especially when his ass was soon stuffed with two fingers.

The stabs of pain continued, even if not as intensely. Although, when Shoju did find a balance between discomfort and relaxation, the pleasurable sensations soon began to make themselves known.

Began to take over, in fact.

"You're so hard, boy." Master Ito announced. Shoju realised the man was fondling his growing hard-on with one hand at the same time he fucked him with the fingers of his other. He was good.

Very good.

"You're the…you're making m-me hard," Shoju stammered.

"I see you like this sort of attention, hmm?"

"I…do."

And it was true. Having his prostate stimulated, milked really, was something else. He couldn't describe it. Shoju could certainly feel the delightfully erotic build-up as he was pleasured in such a way while at the mercy of the master's expert touch.

"It won't be long, now," Master Ito declared. "I can feel

your body tighten and your skin become heated with your desires. It is a truly magnificent thing to witness."

Again, the truth was spoken. Not only was Shoju heading quickly toward the point of no return, like salmon rushing upriver desperately toward their spawning pools, he was indeed flushed and yearning.

Yearning for release.

Master Ito increased his intention, really rubbing his touch over Shoju's prostate. With his balls also tightening, his cock aching with the force of his erection, Shoju then felt that all too familiar ache right at the pit of his stomach. A primal and erotic sensation. A sensation that spread quickly to his toes.

He groaned, beginning to quiver.

"Cum for me, boy." Master Ito began masturbating Shoju with as much effort as he pleasured his prostate. What a rush! Shoju was lost for words, feeling giddy and wonderful and oh, so very heightened as he stepped toward the edge of his climax, no looking back. "Let yourself go. Cum. Cum now!"

Shoju shouted his joy, overwhelming, desperate, and consuming, before he did as instructed. And wow, did he cum! He couldn't believe it. He spurted thick ribbons of his jizz all over the tatami matting between his legs, one, two, three massive jolts of his orgasm delivering it with force.

A moment later, and just as Master Ito removed his fingers, Shoju collapsed into a heap of quivering joy, sweat covered and panting. "Thank…t-thank you…sensei."

"It was my pleasure, Shoju-Kami."

Shoju knew he was utterly spent, having cum four times

now. Simply incredible. And what made it even more amazing, each progressive orgasm was more powerful and profound than the last. Wow.

Who'd have thought?

Master Ito had left the room without another word, his footsteps silent and dextrous. And while Shoju was left there all alone once more, lying on the matting to stew within his own juices still swirling within him, he had to come down from his high without being comforted that time.

Shoju missed that, he admitted.

Although he didn't have time to contemplate such things, because again he once more heard the masters talking outside the room's walls.

"Yes, I believe he is the right choice," Shoju understood Master Ito to say through the miasma of his post-orgasmic state and exhaustion. Whenever he tried to move, even to try and hear better, he shuddered all over—Master Ito was right; a prostate-induced orgasm was something else and then some, wasn't it?

In the end, and for now, Shoju decided to stay as he was, within the bliss of being worshipped.

"Then it's settled," Master Fuoco replied. "He will be the one we'll choose when the time comes."

Master Horo added, "I'll volunteer to prepare him."

"You know what to do?" Master Ito questioned.

A harrumph. "I've been preparing the boys we've selected for such a thing for over ten years. Why would Shoju-Kami be any different?"

Master Vitus snapped back, "You don't normally volunteer, even if you get tasked to do them in the end."

Another noise of dismissal from Master Horo. "You're all just jealous, for as you now know, Shoju-Kami is perfect. Truly perfect."

"Be that as it may, I agree. Shoju is perfect, but he's also very pliable to our needs, too. That's most important. As such, I know he'll please the Kami of the temple now we've made our decision, of that I have no doubts." Master Ito declared. "And seeing as you asked first, Master Horo, you shall be the one named to prepare the boy."

"Thank you, Master Ito," Master Horo replied.

Master Fuoco chimed in, "You have one year to do so. As I'm sure you're well aware, when the choosing season is upon us again, we'll need another honoured to take Shoju's place once his duties have been completed."

Master Ito said, "That is the way of the temple."

"That *is* the way of the temple," Masters Vitus and Fuoco replied in unison.

Master Horo didn't seem to reply.

Mat's mind was a complete muddle of his mixed feelings, from confusion to arousal to doubts. How could Akai carry a baby? And carry *his* baby, no less! Was that what being an

Omega meant? That Akai could get pregnant, even though he was a man?

Surely, that wasn't possible!

But the conversation, and therefore Mat's growing questions, wouldn't be resolved. Not yet, anyway. He was led to a real waterfall, one that towered so high, its peak was obscured by swirling, thick mists. He'd never seen such a natural wonder, one ground-shakingly powerful and awe-inspiring at the same time with its roaring waters and powerful currents beneath it.

"When you said we were going to the waterfall gate, I assumed it was just a pretty name for the thing, not an actual waterfall," Mat observed.

Akai laughed. "Names are a funny thing, aren't they?"

Mat narrowed his eyes. "Yeah, like Omega—whatever that means."

"That name isn't so hard to understand."

"How so?"

Akai shook his head. "I'll tell you everything you need to know when we're truly safe within the secret village. I promise."

"The village of outcasts, you mean."

"Yes, *your* village now," Akai snapped back.

Mat shut his mouth.

With Akai holding Mat's hand, his hard-on raging as well as his thoughts, they went behind the waterfall together.

There was a narrow corridor hewn into the rock behind it, the gap only wide enough for one of them to go through at a time. Akai, obviously knowing this, led the way. Mat noted how he didn't let go, reaching back his arm so they could remain physically connected.

Mat admitted he liked that.

Beyond the corridor, wonder opened up before him. A valley, green and bountiful, greeted his gaze once he'd become accustomed to the light after the darkness of the stone corridor.

But that wasn't the wonder Mat noticed first. *That* wonder was the vegetation itself. Because no sooner had he stepped onto the green, green grass, brilliantly vibrant, than he found himself surrounded by man-sized mushrooms and a myriad of other plants that wouldn't normally get to such a height. What was that about? What's more, the flowers these plants bloomed were massive, truly. How was that possible? To make it even more unbelievable, the insects and bugs crawling, slithering, and flying about everywhere, pollinating and feeding off the monstrous bounty, were mostly the size of house cats.

Some were bigger.

There was even a black flying beetle thing that could have been mistaken for a wolfhound, it was that huge. Mat had to duck as the bug flew overhead, casting a shadow. Amazing.

"What *is* this place?" Mat had to ask, dumbstruck. He let go of Akai's hand.

"It's your home now—and you're safe here. Trust me."

Mat, still dumbfounded, mouth agape and eyes wide, had to ask, "But how…how is this possible?"

Akai shrugged. "How is it possible that the men of this

place are able to bear children?—well, sons, actually. No women are born here."

"Sons?"

"Yes, Matashi. You will put your son into me now that you're my Alpha."

Mat blinked, coming back to the moment as he pulled his gaze away from all that was around him. "About that. I don't know…if I can…"

"Why not?" Akai's expression was puzzled. "Don't you want to fuck the man who loves you?"

Mat stopped dead in his tracks. "Wait…that's a whole lot of stuff to unpack right there." And he did indeed take a moment to consider his next words. When he had done so…for now…all he could come up with was, "And how can you love me? You don't even know me."

Akai, without hesitation, replied, "From the moment I touched you, I knew without doubt you were my Alpha and that I loved you."

"I…can't accept that," Mat admitted. "And it…it doesn't work like that for me. I can't just fall in love with someone at first sight. I'm sorry."

Akai looked Mat in his eyes. "Why are you sorry?"

"I…don't know."

Akai smiled, right to his beautiful blue eyes. "Matashi, listen to me. You *are* my Alpha, and as we get to know each other over the next month, and the cravings you have inside get more powerful, you *will* come to love me. It's how things are."

"But what about Shoju?"

"Was he your lover who was chosen to join the Cult of Men?"

"Yes." Mat felt his cheeks warm. "But Shoju wasn't my lover…not exactly. He was more my companion."

"Did you fuck him?"

Mat was taken aback. "Um…no."

"Did he fuck you?"

Mat shook his head. "No. It…our relationship wasn't like that…not yet, anyway."

A raise of an eyebrow, one revealing Akai's curiosity more than at any other time Mat had known him. "Did you commit yourself to Shoju, then?"

"Only as my friend for life—why?"

"I don't want to get in the way of anything, Matashi. I want you to be my Alpha with no strings attached. That's how it should be."

"What if I don't want to be your Alpha?" Mat folded his arms, somewhat annoyed now even though his body raged with embarrassment because of the course of their conversation.

A course he wanted to steer away from.

Another shrug. "If that's how you truly feel, could you do one thing for me before you make your final decision, though?"

Once more, Mat was surprised. "Of course. You *did* save my life, after all. Name it."

"Give me a month to change your mind."

Mat became curious. "Why a month?"

"Because, as I come to the height of my first heat within that time, I know you'll change your mind. You'll change your mind about everything, in fact." Akai looked down. "The impressive bulge in your fundoshi already tells me that journey has begun."

Mat unfolded his arms, placing his hands on his hips as he was blushed even more, his cheeks almost on fire, he was certain.

But then a new urge came to the fore while under Akai's scrutiny, one that'd been there all along but was finally bubbling up to be noticed. He glared at his saviour with more intent. Without considering his next words carefully, fuelled by his rising lust and his need for Shoju, for anyone, he blurted, "How about I bend you over that mushroom and fuck you right now, then? Get it over and done with, if that's what you want. Save us time, right?"

"If that's what you want, Matashi, I'll lay down for you without hesitation." Akai opened his samue and pulled down his fundoshi to reveal his own erection. Mat gasped as the man's thick uncut cock sprang to attention, already leaking his arousal and revealing without a doubt the truth of his words. "So, please, are you sure that's what you want?"

Mat, amazed and provoked in equal measure, admitted, "I...don't know."

"An honest answer." Akai stuffed his cock back into his underwear before offering his hand once more. "How about we get to know each other first, hey? Then we can make proper decisions together without the feeling of being rushed."

"I think you're right." Mat nodded. "But can you please tell me all you know, as you promised? About this place.

About you. The Omegas who live here. Everything. I want to know everything."

"Of course, it'll be my pleasure."

"But before all that, can we get something to eat and drink? I'm famished after our desperate dash through the forest."

Akai offered a bow. "It would be my honour to do for you whatever you desire, Matashi."

Mat smiled, but nervousness struck him once more as the reality of everything that'd happened finally hit him right where it mattered. In his heart. "How about you don't talk like that? I'm not your master. And also, you can just call me Mat, please. Plain old Mat. That's what Shoju called me."

"Very well…Mat."

Mat took Akai's hand once more. As the jolt of their contact struck him, he groaned deep in his throat. He also shuddered, momentarily breathless and blinded in equal measure. "Oh…I ah…I don't think I'll have to worry about my blue balls for a while."

Akai offered a wide, full grin. "You finally came?"

"I did."

"If you'd asked me, I would have sucked your dick for you ages ago to help you with that."

The uncomfortable, sticky feeling between his legs soon overwhelmed Mat. His cheeks burned for a different reason. Yes, he would certainly need to change his fundoshi before anything else. "Now you tell me."

They both laughed.

But as Mat was led to the secret village, he couldn't help

but think about Shoju even though he knew without doubt now that his body yearned for Akai.

4

Shoju didn't understand what the masters were speaking about earlier. Why would they need another honoured? Wasn't he the one they'd chosen? That thought was soon taken from his mind when all six men entered the private tatami room.

He sat up; at least he felt strong enough to do so.

With a bow, Master Horo announced, "We're all here to worship you as our newly initiated honoured, Shoju-Kami."

"How will you do that?" Shoju asked, curiosity once more burning within him, because what else could they do to him?

He'd passed his three trials.

Right?

Master Horo stepped forward. "While I hold you, because from now on it's my duty to care for you, Shoju-Kami, the other masters will fuck you in turn," he explained. "When they have cum inside you, you'll then be plugged so that the love they've given you will remain inside you for as long as possible."

Shoju, aroused by those words, especially at the

thought of being plugged, too, had certainly found out what else they could do…and then some.

But *all* of them worshipping him like that?

Was he ready? He didn't want to disappoint them. "I'll do my best to take you all," Shoju said.

The men all nodded, smiling.

"I know you will." Master Horo picked up Shoju; his muscles bulged, and he grunted as he did so, even if the action itself seemed effortless. The man was so strong, and Shoju realised he loved being in his arms.

"Then I'm ready," Shoju said as the men began crowding around him while at the same time freeing their stiffened cocks from their underwear.

What a sight!

Master Fuoco interjected, "But only if you want us to give you our love, Shoju-Kami."

Shoju stirred to a stronger arousal as he began to feel the heat of the moment overtake him. "I do, senpai. I do."

Master Horo knelt to get more comfortable, pulling Shoju into him with more intent. The butterflies of anticipation fluttered within Shoju. He also liked that, mostly because he knew he was ready for them to worship him.

"Excellent," Master Vitus said while offering Master Ito a knowing nod.

Shoju didn't know what that was about, but again, before he could contemplate such things, Master Horo grabbed Shoju's legs to pull them apart, really exposing him for what was about to happen.

When obviously satisfied, Master Horo declared, "Our

honoured is ready to receive all of your worship, gentlemen."

There were more nods and grunts of approval from all of them surrounding Shoju. With their eyes widening as they continued to admire him and his growing erection, caressing it and kissing it in turn—paying particular attention to his foreskin, which was also licked with eagerness—Shoju began to get carried away by the moment.

Really let himself go.

Soon, he was trembling delightfully in expectation, moaning and feeling the need to be loved by all of them. Also, unable to help himself, he leant back into Master Horo, heated skin against heated skin, breathing hard, and flexing his arms backward so he could hold the man around his neck.

Shoju felt welcome in Master Horo's embrace.

At that, Master Horo smiled in appreciation, one that sent a shiver all through Shoju. If he wasn't mistaken, he felt a connection to the man then. One deeper than when he'd first met him back in the garden and he'd taken Shoju's hand.

A connection that went beyond the physical.

Then again, he couldn't be sure of that; it had been a momentous and bizarre day already. One that most certainly wasn't over yet—he was about to lose his virginity in a gangbang, after all.

Nothing done by halves, for sure.

But Shoju also wanted to do his best, please them all equally for what they'd done for him: chosen him above all the others as their honoured.

How could he not feel like that?

"Yes, I'm ready," he affirmed, realising he wanted to get on with things already. "Worship me, please. All of you." At that, his insides began churning with his carnal desires, chasing those butterflies away and replacing them with something far more powerful: yearning.

He was already writhing.

Master Fuoco had a bottle of lubricant in hand, drizzling the contents over Master Ito's erection to make it glisten. Shoju liked how they helped each other.

"I'll be the first to fuck you, Shoju-Kami," Master Ito said, once prepared. "As you've realised, I've got the smallest cock. And if we fuck you in the order of our sizes, then you'll be able to endure far more. This will give you a true, hands-free orgasm. And you will fall deeper and deeper into bliss while being worshipped. That is the way of the temple."

"I understand," Shoju said, knowing that Master Fuoco would be the last man to fuck him going by what he'd been told.

"And while they worship your anus and cock," Master Horo whispered into Shoju's ear, "I'll worship your mouth to really keep you excited."

"Will you fuck me too, senpai?"

"Because I'm holding you for the others, I'll have to fuck you later in private, me being your caretaker and all. That is also the way of things."

"Oh yes, senpai." Shoju moved his head so the man could do just that, feeling himself stir even more. "I want you to spit into my mouth and then fuck me with your tongue while the others fuck me with their cocks, Master Horo. I desire it. I do!"

"You are a true treasure, Shoju-Kami," Master Horo replied.

"Agreed," Master Ito added.

The others agreed too, their leering smiles holding while they continued to caress and admire Shoju with their loving touch all over him, more so upon his tightening balls and now fully engorged cock.

Shoju loved it.

But the time for talk was over. And as silence fell, a new kind of energy filled the tatami room.

The energy of lust needing to be fulfilled.

Soon, Shoju felt a delightful pressure between his legs, not painful but no less overwhelming, indicating the worship had begun in earnest as Master Ito penetrated him, his knob slipping into Shoju with a pop.

Shoju moaned. "Fuck me harder!"

Obeying, the man quickly began thrusting and grunting, gripping Shoju's hips for better purchase. And while Shoju was held in such a way, Master Horo gave Shoju what he desired.

"Hmm," Shoju moaned as Horo spit again and again; soon his mouth was awash with the man's tangy saliva. It was truly wonderful. Shoju moaned again, that time for a different reason: his need to be with Master Horo once the others had worshipped him.

During this time, the others indicated their approval once more.

"He truly is our honoured," one of the masters Shoju didn't know said.

Master Vitus replied, "He is, and without a shadow of a doubt, either."

All too quickly—and with Master Horo's mouth now upon him, lips pressed tightly to seal their tender kisses and their tongues dancing the dance of their love, respect, and admiration—Shoju felt Master Ito shudder as he came to his climax inside him.

A strange feeling.

A lovely one too. He'd made the man do that, made Master Ito lose control, just like Shoju had done when he'd sucked the man's cock for the final trial.

Shoju, being honest, loved that sort of power he held over the man, as he would have that kind of influence over all of them, really. He wanted more already. Wanted to be worshipped by all of them in turn, as promised.

He wasn't even close to climax yet.

When Master Horo parted for a moment, Shoju blurted, "Keep fucking me! Fuck me hard, all of you. If I'm going to make *you* cum, make *me* cum too! Please! I don't care if each of you has to cum into me twice for me to get there. I just want to be fucked by all of you and feel the orgasm I'll get as a result of it! *Please!*"

More approval, touching, and fondling, so much so, Shoju felt his cheeks warm and his cock get harder as the men around him increased their vigour and purpose. That was better.

Much better.

All the while, Master Horo continued with his tender,

loving kisses, lubricated by even more saliva while the other men did what they desired. Soon, every last one of them, including Master Fuoco, had given Shoju their love.

They were all now a part of Shoju.

A few of them did indeed fuck him for the second time. But Shoju finally came when they were all done, a little burst that rocked him to his balls, even if not much cum spurted out of his cock. The masters all smiled. Shoju had to admit, cumming for the fourth time was an effort, and he had to concentrate hard to do so. His whole body was sore as a result of it.

His anus, more so.

Master Fuoco was big—his cock had hurt Shoju most of all.

But it was also good.

Sweating, exhausted, and feeling the most satisfied and loved he'd ever felt at any time before, Shoju was done. Truly. Master Horo had helped him get there, for sure. Because without his kisses, Shoju knew it wouldn't have been possible.

"You were magnificent," the man whispered into his ear.

"I can't move, though," Shoju admitted.

Another kiss, long and lingering and delightful.

When Shoju finally parted from Master Horo's kiss, Master Ito inserted the butt plug. "Don't remove this until Master Horo instructs you to do so, Shoju-Kami."

"I won't, sensei."

One by one, the masters left the tatami room, mumbling their compliments. Master Horo placed Shoju on the matting carefully. "You will sleep with me tonight after I have bathed and fed you and seen to your every need."

"Is that when you'll fuck me? Tonight?"

"Yes, Shoju-Kami. If that is your wish."

But Shoju felt a different urge after hearing Master Horo's words. He then realised he was hungry as well as being tired to his bones. "Please, just call me Shoju, senpai."

Master Horo carefully brushed away Shoju's sweat-soaked hair from his forehead, giving him yet another kiss, this time on his cheeks and nose. "Then in return, how about you call me Horo, hmm?"

Shoju nodded, an effort to do so. "I think…I think I love you, Horo—I did so from that first moment you held my hand. I know that now."

"As I love you, Shoju."

"You do?"

"I do. That's why I gladly volunteered to be your caretaker." Horo offered Shoju another kiss, one filled even more with the truth of his words because it was once again placed on Shoju's tender, tingling lips, lovingly so. "And I'll truly look after you for the rest of your days, that much I promise you."

At that, Shoju remembered the whispered conversations he'd caught beyond the walls of the tatami room between the trials today. "As long as I'm the honoured, you mean?"

Horo seemed taken aback. "I don't understand what you're getting at."

"I heard you talking with the other masters," Shoju

explained. "You all said I'd only be the honoured until the next choosing season. What happens to me after that?"

Horo replied, "Whatever happens, I'll protect you with my life. That is all you need to know for now. But also know, I'll never lie to you. You have my word and my honour, Shoju."

Shoju nodded; he trusted Horo. "In that case, can you also tell me what happened to Matashi Soju? Was he chosen for any role within the temple today?"

A look of sadness washed over Horo's pleasant features. "No, he wasn't, I'm sorry. He was named outcast."

Shoju inhaled in a sudden shock that rocked him to his core and quickly became immense sadness. His heart ached as it broke, making him feel hollow and grief-stricken. Poor Mat. His family, too. Poor, poor, beautiful and handsome Mat. The boy Shoju had spent his life with until now.

His companion and promised betrothed.

Not anymore, it seemed.

And whether from the effects of his exhaustion or from everything else that'd happened this eventful day adding heavily to the devastating news, Shoju couldn't help but burst into tears. It came out of him like a levee had been broken.

He wept and wept.

Horo held Shoju for as long as needed, which seemed like forever, as his soul cried with him for his Mat. In fact, Shoju didn't even notice when the man picked him up and carried him toward the temple's bathhouse, placing him into the fragrant warm waters with care and attention.

"Let me wash you while you rightfully keep grieving for your friend, Shoju."

Surprising himself, Shoju said, "You'll never leave me, will you?"

"Not ever, no."

After he'd eaten his fill with delicious foods he'd not had before but enjoyed immensely, drank until quenched, rested, and, more importantly, changed into more appropriate clothing, Mat felt compelled to ask, "I want to know one thing before you explain everything to me, Akai."

"What's that, Mat?" Akai replied, placing another log onto the communal fire in the village square, which they now sat around as evening approached.

They had watched the rising of the new moon, and now there were a few twinkling stars higher in the bruising sky. A lovely night was approaching. Even the cicadas were merry, their noise the background of high summer Mat loved.

"What did you mean when you said the Cult of Men was a sanctioned sex cult with an agenda?"

"You're worried about your friend Shoju, aren't you?"

"I am." Mat had never spoken such truer words.

The few others around the open fireplace grunted their understanding while sipping on their saké or smoking pipe-

weed, even though it was Akai who responded in earnest. "And rightfully so, I fear."

"What do you mean?"

"If he was chosen to be a temple servant," Akai began, "he'd be castrated straight away. Boys having their balls taken in such a way is the ultimate show of obedience and submission." A shift in weight; Mat knew what that was for. He felt it too. "From then, the servant would live in fear of extreme punishment if he didn't perform his duties satisfactorily. It's the harshest life of all, even worse than being an outcast, in my opinion."

"Not for the families of the boys chosen, it isn't," Mat chimed in. "Even if he's chosen to be a servant by the temple's masters."

"That's why the Cult of Men is sanctioned, as I said." Akai spat into the flames in an obvious show of his disgust. "You all let it happen blindly without understanding what goes on behind closed doors; all because families are given gold in compensation for their son's servitude. Makes me sick to my stomach, it does. All those poor boys being blindly led into a life no one would want if they knew the details of the fine print."

Akai again spat into the flames.

Mat, thoughtful about what was said, nevertheless wanted to steer the conversation back on track. Besides, one step at a time, right? "I know Shoju wouldn't be selected as a servant. I know that to my bones."

"Then if he's been chosen to be a temple guard, he'll lead a slightly less uncomfortable life, even if it'll still be full of harsh discipline and endless training. Training that includes sexual humiliation and genital torture if there is any failure to please their task masters. The guards must be tough...and for good reason. They're formidable, terrifyingly so."

Mat nodded, but snorted his amusement all of a sudden. "I don't think they'd choose Shoju for that, either. He was...not exactly warrior material." He didn't elaborate that Shoju was chosen as his companion for a reason: Mat liking the company of men from an early age.

Besides, the gay men of his village were always paired together so they could look after each other—the sooner the better. That was the tradition. So it was with Mat and Shoju.

And yes, even though Shoju was more effeminate in his demeanour than anything, it was his mother who fiercely protected him, ensured Shoju was looked after until he was chosen.

She even did all the work of the household for him because from the day he was born, she'd placed all of her hopes upon her son's shoulders—hopes that he would be chosen for something far greater than a mere guard or lowly servant when he came of age.

Hopes that her own harsh life would be over too.

Because of all of that, and knowing Shoju and how much he tried to please others, even strangers, Mat knew without a doubt he would be named as the honoured this choosing season.

Without a fucking doubt.

"I see."

Akai shuffled closer to Mat, putting his hand on his

knee; Mat immediately felt the erotic effects of such contact, the spark of arousal that transferred from the man and seemed to have an intimate connection to the stiffening of his cock. And wow, did it get hard…again!

"Then," Akai said, "if Shoju was chosen to be the honoured, that's the worst fate of all."

"What? How?"

Mat swallowed hard. "The honoured boy of the season will be used as a sexual object by all of the temple masters. Used over and over again as nothing but a fuck toy. During which time, he'll also be prepared by one of them for sacrifice so that the Kami of the temple will be pleased, gifting great fortunes upon the masters for their so-called 'good work.'"

"You…you lie!" Mat stood, sputtering in shock. "That can't be true!"

Akai grabbed Mat's hand, pulling him back down so he could once more sit beside him. "It *is* true. Why would I lie to you, Mat?"

"But…Shoju."

"Shoju *is* in great danger, it seems."

"Then we've got to go and rescue him," Mat stated firmly, the fear within him even greater than at any other time before, even when he was thrown to the ground beyond the rejection gate. "We've got to."

"Do you know what you're saying?"

The others around the fireplace revealed their shock at Mat's words, one even dropping his drink so it splashed over his shoes.

Mat didn't fully understand—how could he?—but

replied, "Shoju is my companion, and if you want me to be your Alpha, then you *must* help me, Akai. You must." His voice was full of conviction.

And even though that was a blatant attempt at coercion to get what he wanted, Akai didn't seem perturbed. "I'm sorry, but I can't—none of us here can."

Mat turned to look him in the eyes, the brilliant blues of them sparkling with oranges because of the fire's light dancing around him. "Why not?" he asked.

"Because with me being an Omega and you being my Alpha outcast, please take a moment to imagine for one moment what would happen to us now that you know what they do to their own, hmm!"

"I..." Mat now didn't understand again. "I...what would they do?"

"If they didn't kill us on sight, we'd be caged so we could become their battery hens, that's what would happen." Another spit into the fire. "But instead of giving them eggs, we'd be forced to give them our sons. And I can't even begin to tell you what would happen to those poor boys, for they'd be seen as being even lower than the temple servants."

Mat visibly shivered, like ants were crawling all over him. Akai was right; he didn't want to imagine that. "Then...what can we do?"

"I may have another plan...if you trust me."

Mat sat back down. "If I mate with you, you mean?"

"Yes."

Mat snorted. "Good one, Akai." He knew it was his payback for his weak attempt at coercion earlier. He'd tried.

He really had. But in the end, Mat was glad it hadn't worked.

He not only trusted Akai, he found he respected him, too.

"You started it." A full smile accompanied those words.

Mat managed a light guffaw. "I deserved that."

5

"Do you like the taste of it?" Master Horo asked Shoju as the first spoonful of a sweet-smelling miso was offered to him after being blown on to cool it for his lips.

"I do," Shoju replied once he'd swallowed, enjoying the fact that the man was feeding him. It reminded him of what his mum used to do. "It's very tasty, thank you."

After the bath where he was washed and a nap where he was looked over and sung a lullaby to by Horo, Shoju was escorted into a large dining room within the man's spacious home adjacent to the temple.

Once more, tatami matting graced the floor, along with a long black lacquered table with perfectly set out cutlery upon it. There were many cushions to sit on, more than enough for ten guests.

Shoju and Horo were alone.

That was until two temple servants brought in the trays of food once Horo had banged on a gong to alert them to his readiness to eat. They bowed often while quietly setting it all out before Horo and Shoju.

Shoju said, "Thank you," when one of the servants had

finished placing down the feast before him, one of the dishes the soup Horo was feeding to him.

Horo laughed. "You don't have to thank the servants, Shoju."

Shoju didn't understand. "Why not?"

Horo smiled. "You're truly wonderful." A kiss upon his lips then. "But servants are here to serve you without question. Perhaps if one of them takes your fancy or pleases you with his efficiency, you can get him to suck you off or you can fuck him. But only if you desire it."

"Do *you* get the servants to service you sexually, Horo?"

"Sometimes I do." Horo glanced at the servant attending to him. "But not as often as the other masters."

"I don't think I'll do that."

"That's up to you." With a click of his fingers, Horo gained the attention of the two servants. They stood waiting quietly for their next order. "But you can also get them to entertain you once they've performed their duties."

"What do you mean?"

To the servants, Horo commanded, "You'll both get onto the table where you'll then fuck each other for us to watch. And this time I want to see plenty of kissing and cock sucking action as well. If I feel for one moment that you're not getting into the pleasure you're giving each other, you'll both be severely punished."

"Yes, Master," the two servants replied together.

Without another word, the young men disrobed, getting onto the table so they could do as ordered. Soon, the room was filled with the sounds of them kissing and grunting while they became intertwined. Shoju felt himself warm as he witnessed their cocks stiffening nicely when they began what he came to understand as their dinner entertainment.

They really *did* get into it.

When the two servants had ejaculated into each other, the meal also eaten while all that went on, Master Horo said, "Be gone, the both of you!"

The servants, without even bothering to dress, scurried from the room, bowing without turning their backs before they disappeared beyond the servant's entrance to the dining room.

"I've got to say it was an interesting experience telling the servants to do what lovers do while you fed me my dinner, Horo."

"I take it you enjoyed yourself."

"I did." Shoju admitted he liked seeing other men pleasure each other as he liked being pleasured by men. It was a kind of affirmation that what he enjoyed was as natural as any other kind of love.

"Then they'll do that every evening meal for you from now on."

"I'd like that." But Shoju soon felt himself warm as Horo began touching him and planting kisses, tender and beautiful, all over his lips and cheeks. His arousal heightened once more. "But now that I've rested, I want you to fuck me as you'd promised. *I need you*, Horo, that much I know to my bones."

"Then let me take out the buttplug so I can do for you as you desire."

"Yes, please."

Before he knew it, Shoju found himself placed carefully onto Horo's soft futon within his bedroom like he was precious. He supposed he was. And even though the room was spacious and opulent like the rest of his home, that wasn't Shoju's focus.

Quickly, and as he wanted, Horo came over him, overtaking everything else, wonderfully so, as he became Shoju's world. The man was fully naked and completely hard—leaking, too.

Just as Shoju was.

But already he could sense a difference. This wasn't like the trials. Not even the gangbang he got afterward in thanks, either.

It had a different energy.

A different purpose.

Shoju quickly became enamoured by the experience, writhing under Horo, grabbing at him to pull him closer.

Horo smiled.

Unable to help himself at that sight, Shoju sucked in a deep breath of anticipation, his needs consuming him while he looked up dreamily, lovingly, at the handsome man who'd soon give him all of his love and attention.

"I desire you so much, too, Shoju," Horo whispered. "You're perfect. Perfect in every way."

With no words needed in reply—what could be said anyway?—Shoju opened his mouth instead. Horo, understanding the gesture, the way Shoju offered himself, dribbled his saliva, thick and plentiful, to wet Shoju's lolling tongue, which he'd poked out for that purpose.

The heat between them intensified as they began their

dance of love. The electricity surrounding them, too. So awesome.

So powerful, most of all.

Shoju loved how their connection worked. Because why wouldn't he want all of his lover's fluids inside him? At the same time as they passionately kissed, groaning and consumed with each other, more and more saliva added to lubricate the actions, Horo penetrated Shoju.

"Mhm!" Shoju moaned as the man pushed his cock in even more while holding him tightly, kissing him more and more to really love him in the way he should be.

Such passion.

Such bliss!

Horo's love went far beyond worship, Shoju knew. Because while being held and kissed and fucked, getting hotter, the both of them sweating, wetting the sheets, their musk consuming everything, too, he couldn't imagine himself with any other man.

Not even Mat.

And for Shoju to think that was profound.

"Fuck me harder—give me all of your love!" Shoju called, arching his back so Horo could go deeper into him while they were face to face, sharing breaths.

Shoju even wrapped his legs around his lover's back.

Horo, affected as much as Shoju, his voice a hoarse tremble, so sexy, replied, "I went into you so easily, I can't believe it."

"Yes, you did."

Horo stated, "It must be because your ass had already been lubricated by all the others who worshipped you."

Shoju hadn't thought of that. "Then give me all your cum to add to it, please."

"Yes, Shoju."

From there, and for the longest time, the turning of days into nights, Shoju believed, Horo made love to Shoju. Real love that involved the bedclothes being thrown off the bed and all. A love full of stolen breaths, stomachs quivering in delight, of aching erections, dripping tongues, and burst after burst of jizz deep inside and all over Shoju.

While they were together, the both of them came together.

Came many times.

When utterly spent, panting, numb everywhere, Shoju's balls aching and his cock aching more so, Horo held Shoju in his arms. He was caressed while they both cooled. The stench of the result of their love was all that mattered. All Shoju could smell, really.

It was wonderful…and validating.

And it was Shoju who'd done that to Horo.

Horo *was* his man.

Again, the power of such a thought pleased him. "Thank you, Horo," Shoju offered while kissing him in return, feeling content and completed most of all now.

Horo said, "You're all mine, and I'll do everything in my power to ensure the love we have will only ever be for us."

Shoju sat up to look at Horo. "What do you mean?"

Horo, his eyes going watery, said, "I want you to be my husband, Shoju. It's the only way I can truly protect you."

Shoju took in a breath. "Again…I don't understand."

Horo sucked in a breath, his expression turning serious. "It's been planned that you'll be sacrificed to the Kami of the temple before the next choosing season. That's what was discussed when you heard us all talking."

Shoju became shocked. "What?"

Horo held him, bringing him into a tighter embrace, a protective one if Shoju wasn't mistaken. "I cannot live without you. I know that now to my soul. Therefore, as your appointed caretaker and the man responsible for preparing you for this planned sacrifice, I'll use any law I have at my disposal to save you, Shoju."

"By marrying me, you mean?"

"Yes…by marrying you."

Shoju felt at ease because he believed Horo's words. "Then marry me; I won't say no."

"Good." Horo now smiled, warm and honest. "We will do so within the week's end—I'll begin the preparations first thing in the morning."

Shoju felt his heart melt for what Horo was doing for him. The only thing he could say in response was, "Then how about you fuck me again to celebrate our engagement?"

"I would love to do just that."

"I'm really sore, though," Shoju hated to admit. "So, can you be gentle with me this time?"

"I'll always do as you desire, my dear Shoju."

"Thank you. Thank you for everything. Your honesty most of all."

Mat knew he would have to do as Akai asked, eventually. He was already feeling the increased yearning within him, rising more and more with each passing moment. In fact, he felt its desperation clawing at him like an animal trying to free itself from within a cage.

He didn't like it.

As such, Mat hated to imagine what those lust-filled cravings would be like after a week or two of not being satisfied. Would it mean he'd have to walk around with a permanent boner, unable to even function except to eat? Because he also imagined sleeping wouldn't be fun in such a state of arousal as Akai's heat grew.

Half-jokingly, half-seriously, his lust suddenly ruling him, he said, "Then let me take you behind those bushes over there so we can get it over and done with."

Akai looked stunned. "I beg your pardon?"

Mat, not forcefully, but enough to let Akai understand he meant business, demanded, "I've already got the boner, thanks to you touching me all the time. I might as well put it to good use and jizz inside of you instead of me having to do it inside my fundoshi again."

"You're such a romantic, aren't you?"

Mat stood to try and pull Akai up with him. "Maybe I'm just practical."

Akai's expression suddenly turned serious, as if he'd

become upset by what had transpired. The light mood of before dissipated as quickly as the smoke curling up to the heavens from the open fire.

"Fine." Akai stood, too, determination setting on his face. "Take me wherever you want. When we're there, you can bend me over so you can fuck me like I'm nothing but a hole to stick your cock into. I'll be your warm little fuck toy, if that's what you want. Hey, you don't even have to kiss me in thanks afterward. Just do the deed and be done with it, as you say. I'll not complain. Not once."

They both glared at each other.

Mat gulped. He realised his mistake; he'd become ruled by his cock, and as such, he felt like an ass. "Sorry," he said as he heaved a sigh full of his sudden embarrassment. "You didn't deserve that."

"You think?" Akai stormed off, leaving Mat to the judging glares of the other men around him.

Mat sat back down. "I *think* I need a drink."

The next morning, one bright and full of hope—full of love, too, because the last time he was with Horo it was long and slow and wonderful—Shoju, having slept in his man's arms all night, was woken by voices beyond the bedroom.

He sat up but didn't leave the bed.

Through the paper walls, he heard it all. He heard the

defiance in Horo's voice the most. "I told you already, he's not available."

"We want to worship him, Master Horo," Master Fuoco said, his voice hardening as much as his cock no doubt was, Shoju imagined. "He's not all yours to do with as you please."

"Ah, but he is."

"How so?" Master Vitus demanded. "Explain yourself, Master Horo?"

"You named me Shoju-Kami's caretaker, so that's what I'm going to do. Care for him no matter what it takes…to my dying breath if needed. It's in our laws that I can do so; I therefore suggest you consult the good book and look it up if you doubt me."

"We will do that." Another master snorted his derision as the others agreed with him. "But just so you know, Master Horo, we *will* get our cocks into Shoju one way or another, with or without your blessing."

"Not if he's my husband, you won't."

Master Ito said coldly. "And who'll perform the wedding ceremony, hmm?"

"I'll find a cleric, even if I have to go to the village itself to do so," Horo replied. "I *will* marry Shoju so he'll be protected from your wrong decision. Your unfair decision, I might add. That's my promise to him."

A snort from Master Ito. "You've let your little head guide your decisions instead of your bigger one. Such a fool you are, Master Horo. You know you're not to get emotionally involved with any of them—the servants, guards, or even the honoured. Such a fool."

"Is it wrong to fall in love?" Horo countered.

"In this case, it is," Master Vitus added.

There was a shuffling sound. A door being closed. More shuffling. Shoju imagined the masters had left, and none too happy about it, either. From the course of the conversation that he'd eavesdropped on, he understood the other masters would quickly head to the temple's archives to learn what they could do to go against Horo. Well, that's what he believed, anyway.

And why wouldn't they, after what had transpired?

Shoju, remaining silent all throughout the proceedings, holding his breath in fact, wondered how long Horo could keep them at bay. He swallowed hard. Feeling vulnerable, he didn't like Horo's chances of being able to fulfil his promise all of a sudden.

Horo entered the bedroom quietly, looking haggard. "I gather you heard all that, Shoju?"

"I did." Shoju sat up more. He was sore, especially his ass, after all that'd happened yesterday. "Seems you've upset your friends."

"They know I'm right."

"But will that stop them from doing what they want with me? Will it stop them wanting to sacrifice me to the Kami next year when another honoured is chosen?"

"We must leave the temple." Horo moved to hold Shoju tightly, cradling him in his strong arms. "It'll be the only way we can be truly safe together."

"Where can we go?" Shoju asked, genuinely curious and concerned in equal measure. "The village won't be safe for us. The elders there will turn us in at the first opportunity."

"We must go to the secret village of the Omegas."

Shoju had no clue what the man was talking about. "The what?" he blurted as a result.

Horo moved so he could look at Shoju, right into his eyes. "Know this, too, seeing as you *will* be my husband, come hell or high water. I'm not a man who was chosen to be here like you were."

"What are you talking about?" More confusion reigned. "All the men in the temple have been chosen at some stage or another…right?"

"Not all." Horo shifted his weight. "In my case, I was born here."

"I don't understand."

With a tear that formed, falling onto his chin, Horo explained, "I'm the son of an Omega and Alpha couple who were captured long ago. As a result of their capture, I was born here and taken from them as soon as I could walk to be used as the masters of that time saw fit."

"What do you mean?"

"Without going into the details, I learnt from a very early age that planning and patience pay off. Over the years, I secretly poisoned my captors and punished those who abused me. I also helped all of those I could, even if it meant performing another crime to do so."

Shoju, shocked but intrigued, asked, "You helped other honoureds by marrying them?"

"No, not quite." Horo smiled at what was obviously an innocent question, one well-intended but misplaced. "I made sure I became their caretaker so I could fake their deaths."

"How?"

"I don't want to talk about that."

Shoju became concerned. "If I'm going to be your husband and spend the rest of my days with you, then you need to tell me everything…please. There must be no secrets between us."

Horo nodded. "You're right, of course."

With a deep breath of resolve, Horo told how he had worked his way up the temple's ranks to become a master so he could make a difference, including the day he was finally accepted and had been circumcised to remind him of it. A day he despised because the other masters had leered at him while he bled. Fondled him to try and make him hard while laughing in his face, too. But most of all, he spoke to Shoju about his greatest shame. Because to get where he got as a respected and trusted master of the temple, Horo, even at a tender age, had to debase himself as well as sexually please the men he wanted something from.

But please them, he did.

As such, he quickly got to his goal. The goal of being able to save others from the evil men of the temple who call themselves masters. The ones who were supposed to protect others, especially those working for them, but instead used their positions of power for their own personal agendas.

Shoju understood all too well how power made someone feel. It made him feel good. But he could see how it would go to people's heads if given too freely or without consequences.

Or both.

Horo even told of how he saved the honoured chosen for sacrifice by slaughtering pigs to fool the masters into believing they were dead, always covering the bodies with funeral shrouds so he could get away with it. No one ever checked. Why would they? The deed was done as far as everyone else was concerned.

But even more surprisingly, Horo spoke about how he protected his house's servants from castration and a terrible life of servitude.

"I didn't even know they got castrated." Shoju said.

"Yes, they are. And the two who served us our dinner and entertained us are friends of mine because of what I've done for them—but we also must play our master and servant roles at all times."

"You're a good actor, Horo."

"I have to be," Horo admitted. "And I only order them about in the way I do so as not to arouse any suspicion if anyone overheard." He chuckled. "Everyone seems to hear everything in this house."

"I get that." And Shoju did understand because he sensed Horo cared for the house servants, even before such a thing was revealed. Why else would he get them to make love to each other? He could have ordered them to do anything else.

"They are lovers, too, you know," Horo chimed in to answer the question without needing to be asked.

They really were connected on a deeper level. "That's awesome." Shoju had a thought. "Will they come with us?"

"They must, otherwise they'll be killed as punishment for my defiance."

"Then call them and tell them."

"I take it you're agreeing with me, and we're leaving the temple together?"

"We are." Shoju kissed Horo. "But you've got a lot more to tell me."

"In good time. For now, we must be quick, for I fear we don't have much time."

"I hear that." Shoju then had a sadder thought. "What happened to your mum and dad?"

"My two dads, you mean." But before Shoju could offer a quizzical look and ask for an explanation, Horo continued, "An Omega is a man who gets pregnant by an Alpha, who's another man. I was born from their 'mating,' as they call it, but it's really a deep bond of love. I'm the result of their love."

"That's so sweet."

"I wish it ended that way. Ten years ago, when I became a master after coming of age, my present was to witness them being beheaded."

"Oh…by the gods!" Shoju felt his tears well as much as Horo's had, affected by what he was told more than he could believe. "I'm so sorry."

"That's why I do what I do. For them."

"You are truly an honourable man, and I'd love for nothing more than for you to be my husband."

"Thank you, Shoju." Horo kissed Shoju's hands tenderly. "You know, I still see their faces. But most of all, from the moment I saw you, I see you in them. Your spirit, I mean."

"Is that why you love me?"

"One of the many uncountable reasons, yes."

At that moment, the two house servants entered the bedroom, both of them carrying leather bags and bundles wrapped in cloth.

Horo snorted a laugh. "I take it you heard all that like always, my dear Shin and Itsuki?"

They both bowed. "We did, Horo," one said; the other added, "And we've packed your things so we can make a quick escape with you as soon as you're ready."

"Well done." Horo got up to embrace them. "And thank you, my friends. Thank you."

"You don't need to do that," the first said. "You know we'd do anything for you after what you've done for us."

"I know, Shin. But It's always nice to be told, right?"

Shin bowed again.

The other, obviously Itsuki, added, "We know how the other servants are treated."

"I wouldn't wish that kind of treatment on my dog," Horo expanded.

Shin and Itsuki went to Shoju.

After bowing again, Shin said, "We're honoured to serve you, Shoju, betrothed to Horo and honoured in more than name."

Shoju was at a loss, but managed, "Let's just get out of here so we can all be safe."

"The best way will be through the kyozetsu," Itsuki said. "No one goes near it if they can help it."

Horo nodded. "Good idea."

Without delay, Horo grabbed Shoju's hand while Shin and Itsuki led the way, avoiding open areas and places where temple staff gathered. Before he knew it, he found himself in the sweltering and steaming forest beyond its walls—in complete contrast to the organised and manicured beauty of the temple and its gardens.

And before Shoju could ask which direction this secret village was, the place where men got pregnant by other men, so amazing because he then wished—almost jealously—that he could have Horo's baby, a bell tolled loudly in alarm, frightening him to his bones.

There was shouting too.

"We've got to go!" Horo pulled Shoju as Shin and Itsuki bolted into the undergrowth. "They've found out we've escaped already!"

Shoju didn't have time to panic anymore because he was soon running with Horo as fast as his legs could take him through tangled vines, thick undergrowth, and prickly bushes that grabbed at his robe to try and slow him. He couldn't believe this was happening. As if to make matters worse, the shouting seemed to be getting louder too!

Shoju ran with a newfound determination.

His survival.

Mat sat for the longest time in front of the dying fire before he resigned himself to the fact that no one was going to offer him a drink because he'd been such a jerk. He got that.

Sighing to no one in particular, he said, "Looks like I'm heading to bed then, hey?"

A grunt from the man who'd dropped his drink earlier was his reply. The others didn't even look at him. Mat understood their coldness. He hadn't exactly treated Akai with any respect, something he knew he had to address…and fix. He certainly didn't want to disrespect anyone, the beautiful man who saved him, least of all.

Approaching Akai's home, Mat entered without knocking. "Are you in here, Akai?" he called.

No answer.

He crept through the darkened house to Akai's bedroom, trying to avoid knocking into any furniture. Why was it big toes were great at finding any jutting corners of couches or legs of tables in the dark? He pushed open the bedroom door; it creaked too loudly.

"You make so much noise, the villagers on the far side of town could hear you," Akai said.

"Sorry…did I wake you?"

"No."

Mat approached the bed. The curtains were open, so the gloom of night that reached into the room gave him something to see by. Akai was atop the bed clothing, arms folded behind his head. He'd clearly been contemplating recent events. Mat would have done the same if the situation were reversed.

"Can I join you?" Mat asked hopefully, more so as an added sweetener to his apology.

"Why?" Akai snapped. "You'll only get an erection you won't know what to do with."

"I deserved that, too."

"You did." Akai sucked in a breath, one full of his emotions, if Mat wasn't mistaken. "Can you tell me what you're afraid of, Mat."

Mat, thinking about the question, sat on the bed. Akai reached over to touch him, no doubt to comfort him. The man was amazing, really. Even now, when Mat had proven he was an ass, Akai still cared for him.

He decided to amend his mistakes.

Before the contact was made, Mat acted, grabbing Akai's hand first to hold it tightly, kissing it, too. He enjoyed the stirring inside he got from their closeness, he realised. And wow, did he have a hard-on that could gag a village donkey right about now.

Akai melted into a smile.

"I told you, it's my defeatist personality shining through. I mean, why would anyone want me, let alone want to have my son?"

"Shoju wanted you, didn't he?"

"He did."

"Then how is it difficult for you to believe I want you, too?"

Mat looked Akai in his eyes, and even within the dimness inside the bedroom, he could see the blues of them glinting hopefully. "Can we start again?"

"What do you suggest?"

"How about we...comfort each other first? Take it one step at a time before we actually...you know...mate."

"You do know any penetration on your part will result in a pregnancy because you're my Alpha, don't you?"

"Yes, I got that. If I fuck you, we'll be overwhelmed by sleepless nights, dirty diapers, and feeding times at all hours nine months later." Mat shifted his weight but held his grip within Akai's, loving it now, in fact. He also became giddy under the man's influence, new urges overtaking him. "But I didn't mean that sort of comfort."

"Well...what did you have in mind, then?"

"You...you can fuck me, right?"

Akai seemed taken aback. "I...I never considered an Omega being the one who would penetrate his Alpha. It's not how things are done. An Omega is always the uke. Always."

"Who says so?"

Akai sat up, surprise on his face. "It's just the way it is."

Mat shuffled closer, placing Akai's hand on his bulge. "I want you to fuck me, Akai. I want you to jerk off my cock while you're inside me to make me cum for you. Is that too much to ask of you for us to begin our relationship, something that should be a two-way street and not all one-sided, anyway?"

"I didn't know you thought like that."

"How could I not when, from the first moment I saw you, you talked of bonding and mating and me being the one to give you my son? It was all kinds of serious and full on, you've got to admit."

A moment of pause. "I can see how you thought as you did. I'm sorry. I shouldn't have come on so strong."

"And I shouldn't have been an ass about it," Mat admitted. "So, as I said, let's start again, hey?"

Akai smiled. "Then I'd better get the lube so I can fuck you and be your seme, Mat."

"Now you're talking."

Akai, after retrieving the lubricant from the bedside table, came to give Mat a kiss. It was sweet, gentle, and dry. A mere ghosting of lips, really. Far different from Shoju's; his were always passionate and full of moments where he stabbed his tongue dripping with saliva into Mat's mouth while at the same time trying to suck his lips off his face. Not that there was anything wrong with that.

But he enjoyed Akai's kiss the most.

As such, Mat felt compelled to add, "Please tell me what you want me to do for you, Akai. I want to be your submissive tonight as well as your uke."

"This is so strange."

"But hot, right?"

An enthusiastic nod. "Indeed."

"Then I'm at your command." Mat really was aroused now, so much so, he could feel the heat and connection growing between them as much as his aching cock.

"Okay…take off your clothes for me," Akai said timidly, clearly not used to being in control—obviously such a thing wasn't a part of his training.

Mat almost laughed. "Say it like you mean it."

Akai cleared his throat, sitting up straight. "Get your

clothes off now, or I'll spank you for being a naughty boy for not doing as you've been told!"

"Oh, fuck!" Mat gasped. "That was hot, Akai!" He felt his cheeks burn, head spinning, too. "And where the heck did *that* come from?"

Akai looked as shocked as Mat felt. "I…don't really know. Was it too much?"

"Who cares?" Mat then smiled wickedly as his thoughts, already a rush of his desires, went to a more carnal place. "And it wasn't too much at all. In fact, I want you to spank me now. Spank me until you turn my butt bright red so it becomes like a painted target for your cock."

"You *want* me to do *that?*"

"Yes," Mat breathed as his heart began racing, as he began breathing heavier, too.

"Then how about you…um, lay across my legs so I can begin?"

Mat shivered with delight, hanging on every moment. "You're making me so hard right now, you have no idea."

"Also, I want you to pull up your robe after you've removed your fundoshi for me."

"Yes, Akai."

A heartbeat or two later, naked and eager, Mat was sprawled across Akai's legs, his bare buttocks at the man's mercy. Mat loved it, the feeling of being under someone else's control. As such, he writhed and moaned as he built himself up for what was to follow, ensuring he rubbed his aching, throbbing cock against Akai's inner thigh as well, his foreskin helping lubricate his actions along with his oozing pre-cum.

Akai must have appreciated that. "You're very hard, aren't you?"

"It's all because of you and what you're doing for me, Akai."

"Then I won't waste any more time."

Before Mat could reply, the first strike of Akai's hand found him. The result was a loud thwacking sound that shocked him more than the actual contact, which he found he liked.

"Ahh!" was his automatic reaction as he began to slip into the role required of him—the role he realised he desired.

Akai seemed to stop. "Was that too hard? You sounded like it was too hard."

"No…keep going. Keep going!" Mat writhed with greater purpose, enjoying himself more than he would have ever imagined. "Really get me worked up so I'm soon begging for you to fuck me."

"I don't want to hurt you."

"You won't. I'll tell you if you get too hard."

"Promise."

"I promise."

Akai spanked and spanked; each time the sting of his contact combined with his arousing influence because of his growing heat, it blew Mat's mind. "Oh GOD, yes!" and "That's it! Spank me harder!" were common words blurted from his gasping, open mouth many times, his tongue dripping with his lust as much as his cock.

Akai didn't disappoint.

Harder and harder, Akai spanked Mat, as desired. As

needed. Between longer sets, he even rubbed Mat's buttocks gently, soothing the tortured skin, before starting again. Mat couldn't believe how good it all felt. How arousing. How overwhelming, too.

He was wrecked by the time Akai asked, "Is that enough?" Wrecked in the best possible way.

"Yes, it's enough. Please fuck me now!" Mat was panting, sweating, too. "I need you to cum inside me so you can mark me as your Alpha," he blurted while in the heat of the moment.

"Err…that's not how it works, Mat," Akai replied without delay.

For an instant, the mood was broken. Mat needed to get it back before the damage was permanent. "It's how *we* work…okay?"

"Oh…okay." Akai moved so he could lay Mat onto the bed proper, coming over him quickly. "Gosh, your cock has leaked so much."

"More than my butt's sore from your spanking, that's for sure."

"See? I didn't spank you too hard, did I?"

"No, you really didn't," Mat admitted because it was true. "I loved it. Now lube up that thick cock of yours and shove it deep into me…please, Akai. I'm going to burst here at any moment, I know it!"

A smile as Akai lubricated his ample length. "I love it when you talk like that."

"And I love it when you take control." Mat opened his legs for his man, as wide as he could. "Now *please* fuck me for the love of all things holy!"

"With pleasure!"

Mat was quickly engulfed by a different sort of lust: the warm feeling that only happened when he knew he was a part of another. An important part. And sure, at first their coupling hurt, even though plenty of lube was slicked over the important parts of the both of them. How could it not? Akai was well endowed. But that didn't matter.

Not at all.

What mattered was that they were building a relationship, one Mat could understand far better than he seemed to grasp Omega and Alpha dynamics. And that was everything to him.

"You're my first," Mat said while Akai seated himself properly within Mat after a few fumbles, stalls, and reddening cheeks complete with shy turn-away glances.

"As you are…mine."

"Then let's walk this journey of discovery together."

"Yes."

Mat, to his growing delight, discovered Akai fucked like he kissed; it was almost like an apology. So sweet. Mat couldn't help but become enamoured even more as Akai's gentle pushing, loving embrace, and tender, ghost-like kisses consumed him while they both trod the path to their climaxes together.

Mat wouldn't last long, either.

And this time, he didn't encourage Akai to change his methods. The way he made love, soft and silent, gentle, too, was perfect. Exactly what Mat needed after the intensity of earlier.

Before too long, Akai grabbed Mat's face, planting

more loving kisses before whispering. "I think I'm going to cum now."

"You didn't last long," Mat replied, not as a judgement but as an observation.

"You feel so good…I can't help—ah!" Akai shuddered for a moment, his face brightening along with a deeper colour flooding his cheeks. "I'm sorry, I couldn't hold back. Your ass was so tight and warm and…and it really did feel good to be inside you."

Mat, feeling Akai's cock pulse while still inside him, became overwhelmed. It was weird how their connection seemed to be synchronised. Because, to his surprise, he, too, came after Akai completed his orgasm and collapsed onto him, holding him tightly.

But Mat's climax wasn't gentle.

"Oh, fuck!" he said with a sharp hiss, quivering and shuddering underneath Akai, the weight of the man pressed against him, heightening everything.

He came and came.

The action was almost a convulsion, as if a demon had possessed him and now wanted out because an exorcist's prayer had commanded it. He'd felt nothing like it in his life. Nothing.

"Oh…my fucking god!" Mat yelled with the final burst.

All too soon, he was spent. An awesome feeling. Not only was he flushed, hot, and panting, feeling exhausted after being drained to his balls, he held Akai with as much intention as he received.

They stayed in their embrace for an eternity.

Or enough time for Mat's legs to get their feeling back,

anyway. During which time, Akai offered more kisses. Mat reciprocated, but encouraged their connection to go deeper.

He needed it to.

Akai seemed to understand. And quickly, he gently pushed his tongue to part Mat's lips in understanding. It was brilliant. The action alone of that simple connection was something that sent shivers all through Mat.

What's more, the oozing warmth of Mat's ejaculation became the greater glue between them. That, and the fact Mat realised Akai hadn't pulled out of him yet.

"You're...still hard," Mat observed—or rather felt.

"I want to cum inside you again."

Mat smiled. "Then please do."

Their second time was just as wonderful as their first. They also came together. After which, Akai moved so he could lick up the cum from Mat's stomach; tickling him with his tongue sent just as much arousal through him as any other time he'd touched Mat. He could tell his heat was intensifying as a new day dawned.

"I could spend the rest of my life with you," Mat admitted.

"Me too."

Mat looked Akai in his eyes. The love there was as clear as day. He knew that because he felt it, too. "I really appreciated what you did for me, Akai. And I feel a lot better about us, truly."

"I now completely understand." Akai wiped his mouth of Mat's cum, licking the back of his hand afterward to savour the taste once more. "But even though it was good for the both of us, such methods won't satisfy us for long.

The urges within us will still grow until we've mated properly and I've become impregnated."

"I know." And it was true. Because even though Mat had ejaculated twice while he'd been loved and treated as he'd wanted to be, at the same time, deep inside, the fires still roared. "And the next time we lay down together, I *will* mate with you."

Akai seemed relieved. "Thank you."

"And after I've given you my son, we can get back to you being in control. You're a natural, and I really enjoyed what you did."

"Me, too…and I'd like that as well."

Mat then laughed. "It's funny."

"What's funny?"

"How Shoju was my companion, and he'd never, not in a million years, do what you did for me tonight, Akai."

Akai kissed Mat's heated lips. "I gave you your deepest desires and your ultimate fantasy, didn't I?"

"You really did."

"Now I know what held you back before. It wasn't your defeatist personality, but your fear that you'd never be fully satisfied in a relationship. Am I right?"

Mat nodded. "You know you are."

"Then let me hold you while you sleep."

"You know, I wouldn't want it any other way."

The morning came quickly, crisp and sunny and beautiful as the night had been, but for a different reason.

Mat loved waking in Akai's arms.

"Good morning," Akai greeted as soon as Mat stirred and opened his eyes.

"I take it you enjoyed yourself last night, then?"

"How could I not?"

Mat held Akai close to him. "Can I ask you something?"

Akai moved so he could look at Mat. "Of course."

"Is there a good time to...you know...mate with you? For the best result, I mean. No...I don't mean that. I mean...for—"

"Any time during my heat cycle is a good time."

"So...you're ready now?"

"I am."

Mat felt his cheeks warm. "Then...seeing as we're working on this two-way street thing between us, I've been thinking about how I want to give you what you desire after you gave me what I desired. It's only fair, right?"

To Mat's surprise, Akai said. "It doesn't work like that."

"What do you mean?"

"*My* desire is to be with my Alpha. Nothing more. Nothing less. It'll be *you* who decides when you're ready to mate."

"Oh...I see."

"To put it simply, I'm available for you right now, and that's all there is to it. If you want to take that step, here I am."

"But..." Mat sat up to run his hands over Akai's hairless chest, liking how his nipples were as hard as his morning glory. As he was, too, thanks to their physical closeness. "How do you feel about being pregnant once I've mated with you?"

"It's the result of my desire, not the cause of it. But if

you're asking if I want to have your son, the answer is a definite yes. Yes, I *really* do."

"Then I want to mate with you right now instead of later."

Akai groaned deep from his throat. "You mean that?"

"I do."

"Then I'm yours, my beautiful and handsome Mat."

Mat felt nervousness and joy, filled with his consuming love for Akai. Wonderfully so. And in a far different experience than last night, one more about completing a duty even if the gentleness and caring remained, Mat moved so he could penetrate Akai.

To his surprise, nicely so, after he'd pulled back on his foreskin and used the lube, his cock slipped in easily after the pop of his swollen knob pierced Akai's anus. In truth, Akai wasn't as tight as he imagined. Was that an Omega thing?

He wasn't sure.

All he knew, as he sunk deeper into his man, was that he became blinded by the rush as he grappled Akai's body to pull him closer, wanting to share his warmth and kisses in equal measure. The overwhelming feeling of connection imbued with Akai's arousing affect spurred him on even more.

Together they groaned and writhed, rolling over the bed wildly as their passion grew and grew, kicking off pillows and bed clothing, intertwined, kissing, thrusting, and clawing at each other's backs.

Akai seemed to get hotter and hotter with each passing

moment. At first, Mat was concerned, but after he realised his lover was enjoying himself, he didn't worry anymore.

"You're so…big," Akai said between kisses, flushed and sweating, his manly smell intoxicating.

"I'm not going to last long," Mat admitted.

"Then cum for me—squirt your load deep in me to give me your son!"

"Oh, fuck, yes!"

And with that encouragement, Mat blew his load with almighty shudders and while pressing passionate, needing kisses, deep and wanting, within Akai's mouth. He became consumed, not only by Akai's heat, but by his own relief as well.

It was over all too soon, really.

They held each other again for ages, like they'd done last night. Mat finally pulled out of Akai, noticing he'd cum as well. "You orgasmed the same time as me, hey?"

"I did."

Mat kissed Akai once more, that time with a different intention. "I love you, Akai. I realise that now. I love you with all my heart."

Akai's eyes blinked rapidly for a moment, watering, too. "I…I love you too, Matashi Soju. I love you so much." He then began to softly weep tears of his obvious joy.

Mat cried too.

Together, both emotional wrecks as they shared breaths and loving glances, they embraced again, holding each other unlike any time before. Like they were both each other's soul. Mat not only had a lover in Akai, he had a partner who would help him rebuild his family, a family that would be raised with love and without fear of the temple's evils. And that affected him the most of all.

He wasn't a failure.

Not at all.

But just as he contemplated that deeper, a new concern found him. "Did you have a plan about how we can rescue Shoju?"

"I do."

Mat knew it. "Then tell me, silly," he replied, while pinning Akai to the bed playfully. "Don't keep me waiting."

"I've organised a guide named Kale to take us into the mountain pass. From there, we can enter the temple of the Cult of Men via a secret entrance."

"There's always a secret entrance to those sorts of places, isn't there?"

Akai looked thoughtful for a moment, which looked kind of funny considering his eyes were still wet from his emotions. Red-rimmed, too. "You know, you're right—I never thought of that."

"Anyway, when do we set out for this pass with Kale?"

"As soon as you've fucked me again."

Mat raised an eyebrow. "I thought…aren't you impregnated now?"

"Sure. But that doesn't mean I don't enjoy being fucked as much as you enjoy it, now does it?"

"Oh…I see." Mat felt his embarrassment. "Then, yes, of course, I'll do that. I would love to."

"That's good." Akai kissed Mat's nose. "You had me worried there for a moment."

Mat felt himself stiffen once more. Akai really did have

that effect on him, even after they'd mated and he sensed his heat had subdued somewhat.

His feelings for him didn't diminish, though. "Now come here, big boy, and let me have my way with you again."

"Oh, yes!"

After they'd made love—did it twice more, in fact, with Mat fucking Akai, and Akai fucking Mat in turn—they bathed together. From there, they shared breakfast, a simple dish of tasty rice and white fish. Delicious. Mat realised he was famished and heartily ate all that was prepared for him. Then he asked for seconds. Then thirds.

"You *did* work up an appetite, didn't you?" Akai said.

"I don't know how!" Mat joked.

They both laughed.

As Akai was packing away the dishes after washing them, Mat offering to help but being told to stay seated while the coffee was made, there was a knock on the door.

"Come in, Kale," Akai called without turning from his chores.

Within a heartbeat, a tall and solidly built man with mysterious eyes, dark and foreboding, came into the room.

Akai bowed respectfully to greet him.

"Pleased to meet you, Kale. My name's Matashi, but you can call me Mat."

Kale bowed, too. "Are you both ready?" the man asked without standing on ceremony or reciprocating the salutation.

Mat didn't know what to make of that. Not until Akai whispered into his ear, "He's in heat. He also hasn't made the pilgrimage to the temple village yet to find his Alpha for his own reasons, so he's going to be a bit tetchy until he does."

"Ah." But then Mat was curious. "I didn't sense that from him, though. Is that…normal?"

"That's because you've mated—you'll only sense me from now on."

"Oh."

To Kale, Akai said, "We're ready, my friend."

Kale nodded. "Let's go, then." He turned, leaving the room as quickly as he'd arrived; his presence may have lasted only a short time, but it was profound, no doubt.

"What if he doesn't find his Alpha?" Mat had to ask when Akai picked up a bag he'd prepared for their journey, one that mostly contained food and water in glass bottles. Although Mat noticed he'd slipped the lube in there too.

He found it quite arousing that Akai believed they'd have time for intimacy during their journey. He didn't mind, either.

"He'll feel the pain of not being completed until he does."

"And what about you, Akai?"

"My heat is over."

And it was true; Mat couldn't sense that lovely arousing tingle to his cock that hardened it every time he touched Akai. Now he got a different sensation, one more about love than anything else.

He liked that most of all.

"You're pregnant, then?"

"I am."

Mat smiled, right to his heart. "I can't believe I'm going to be a father."

"Believe it."

From there, hand-in-hand with Akai, hope within him for their future, the thought that Shoju would be saved, too, if they could manage it—which he hoped they did—they followed Kale beyond the walls of the secret village into the thick abundant forest.

Although Mat forgot how uncomfortable it was being out in the wilds and in nature's abundance. "I'm glad my ass crack is being flossed by my fundoshi, otherwise there'd be sweat to the back of my balls, it's that hot and humid out here."

"I agree." Akai laughed.

"What's so funny?"

"I was only imagining licking the sweat off your big balls."

Mat felt himself warm, right through his cheeks, too. "Ooh, I like how you think, Akai. So naughty!"

"But of course, not before I've had my way with you," Akai added with more gentle laughter. "Because if there's one thing I've learned from last night, I absolutely loved seeing your spanked butt cheeks and my cum dribbling out of your freshly fucked ass. It turned me on, I found."

"Oh wow, I *really* like how you think."

"Less talk, more walking," Kale blurted with a snort as he glared at them from up ahead, frowning so his brows knitted.

Mat, though hard because of Akai's dirty talking and wanting him to take him behind the nearest bush to fuck him good and proper like the gentlemen he was, replied, "Sorry, Kale. We'll talk less and walk more from now on."

Another snort from their guide. "Walk quicker."

Akai shrugged, beaming a mischievous and dirty grin.

Mat couldn't help but try to suppress his amusement…and his arousal. He failed on both counts. Soon they both laughed, much to Kale's annoyance. His hard-on didn't abate, though. In fact, it got worse as he thought about Akai more and more.

Thought about the things they'd do to each other.

But Kale was right. They had a job to do. As such, the rest of their time walking at a stern pace to and then through the mountain pass was uneventful.

Uneventful except for the time Kale allowed them to rest for a minute, and instead of eating something as they should have done, noon approaching fast, Mat and Akai ate each other's cum after swapping quick blowjobs away from Kale's prying eyes.

"You tasted so good," Akai said while guzzling on a bottle filled with water taken from the pool that they'd found themselves at, its waters clear and refreshing against the heat and humidity.

Watching his Adam's apple bobbing while he swallowed kept Mat interested, that's for sure. "Will we have time to fuck?" he felt compelled to ask, those urges consuming him once more.

Before Akai could answer, a throat cleared. "We must get going if we're to be at the temple during the afternoon prayers and while the guards are distracted," Kale announced as he came into view, his foreboding shadow cast over Mat to make him shiver from the sudden coolness he experienced as a result.

Akai shrugged again. "I think that's a no, Mat."

"I got that."

They could soon hear the temple's bells clanging through the haze between the ancient trees as they approached. Kale walked with a lower stoop, seemingly nervous.

Mat knew why.

They couldn't be seen. If any of the stories Akai had told him were true, about how they treat Omegas and Alphas if captured most of all—and he didn't doubt they were probably worse in reality—Mat had to be on high alert.

They all had to be.

"The secret entrance is about a hundred metres from the rejection gate." Kale pointed to where he wanted their attention directed. The looming walls of the temple were now in sight as they inched closer to their goal. "To the left there."

"I don't see anything," Mat offered, speaking the truth. All he could see were forest and walls...and that damn rejection gate. One he wished he could destroy.

Perhaps he would.

A groan from Kale. "If you could see it, it wouldn't be a secret entrance, would it?"

Akai shook his head. "It's all right, Kale. We're all just anxious, that's all."

Kale seemed to calm. "Sorry, Akai. I didn't mean to be blunt with your Alpha...but I don't think he understands the weight of the situation here."

"I do understand," Mat snapped. "How could you think I don't?"

"Because you're more interested in what your cock's been doing during our journey here than getting on with the task at hand."

That hurt. "I'm sorry if you feel that way about me, Kale. But you're wrong. I understand everything."

"We shall see."

Akai said, "Mat is right. He understands. So let's not discuss this any further. We need to work together if we're going to have any chance of success. Right, Kale?"

Kale sighed. "You're right."

"Good," Akai said as he grabbed Mat's hand. "Then let's get to that secret entrance then and get this over and done with, hmm?"

Mat loved it when Akai took control.

Kale stood.

No sooner had he done so, withdrawing his knife in preparation, when he was grabbed by two men wearing temple armour who made themselves known from behind two large trees. Kale yelped, but was silenced by a rough hand over his mouth.

Mat spun on his heels, his heart racing as the reality of what had happened struck him. All he could think about was Akai. He pulled him in closer, knowing he would protect him as best he could to his dying breath; he knew so without doubt.

But his hopes, as small as they were, didn't last long.

Once Kale was subdued properly with a blow to his head, the crack of the weapon against the back of his skull sickening, they were quickly surrounded; more than twenty guards stared at Mat and Akai with their hate. Their lust for blood, really.

Mat realised he was defenceless.

A tall man with a leering glare—clearly a temple master, no one else would hold such arrogance—approached through the crowd of his guards. "Well, well, what do we have here? An outcast and his two Omega friends with delusions of rescuing his companion—I assume that's why you're here, isn't it, Matashi?"

Mat recognised the master.

He was about to answer Master Ito in the most vitriolic way he could imagine when the man raised his hand. At that, Mat was pulled away from Akai, their separation tangible, only to have his mouth covered as he was forced to his knees. Actually, he was quickly gagged with a cloth tied tightly around his head. It was done so roughly it hurt.

He noticed Akai was treated the same.

Master Ito continued, "You've failed in your rescue attempt, Matashi. As Shoju has failed us just as spectacularly."

Mat gulped while being held roughly by two guards. He wanted to tell the arrogant jerk to go fuck himself, but couldn't. Pity. It would have given him some satisfaction.

"Remove his gag," Master Ito said. "I'll allow you to answer me. For now."

"Go fuck yourself." There! He'd said it.

It did make him feel better.

"You first, Matashi." A moment of pause as the man slid his katana from its sheath, the hissing of its metal sickening. "But just so you know, before I cut your head from off your shoulders for what you've done, understand that you were never going to be chosen."

"What are you talking about?"

"Being Shoju's companion, we couldn't risk having you here interfering with his indoctrination. So you see, you would have never been chosen."

"My brother wasn't anyone's companion. Why'd you reject him, then? Hasn't our family suffered enough under your tyranny?"

"Your brother went mad from the herbs we burn within the brazier to calm the candidates. He attacked his choosing master…but then sadly took his own life. Such a shame. He had far more potential than you ever did."

"You're a filthy liar." Mat spat. "More like he didn't want to be your fuck toy like how you're trying to make Shoju one, and you got rid of him like you tried to get rid of me."

"Oh, didn't you know," Master Ito cooed. "Shoju and his caretaker escaped the temple with their house servants early this morning. You just missed them. Again, what a shame you didn't cross paths. It would have saved you a lot of bother. Isn't it delicious how fate works, hmm?"

Mat looked up, hate in his eyes as he glared daggers at the man who held the instrument threateningly. "What?"

"You heard—I don't repeat myself." The man readied the sword, grabbing it firmly in both hands. "Say whatever prayer the outcasts utter to their foul gods. I'll make this as quick as I can for you. For your Omegas too."

"Only Akai is my Omega." Mat tried to reach for his

lover, his heart aching as he yearned to touch him once more. He knew he'd failed him. And not only him, but his unborn son, too.

Master Ito slid his oily gaze to Akai, sneering at him in disgust once he must have realised something. What that was, Mat didn't know.

He didn't care either.

"Then I'll enjoy cutting out his womb where your son grows to show him it before killing him. I'll enjoy that the most of all," the man finally said.

Mat then knew.

"You fucking cunt!" he screamed. "If you so much as lay a finger on him, I'll—"

Mat was struck on the back of the head. "Oof!" He found the dirt, spitting it from his mouth moments later.

"Such bravery you have," Master Ito cooed victoriously. "But it will do you no good. You will die here today."

Mat looked up, his head pounding.

The blade glinted.

"I'm so sorry I failed you, Akai," he mumbled through his pain, physical and otherwise. "You too Shoju. Seems it's my lot in life after all, to be nothing but a failure to those I love."

"You are correct," Master Ito said, almost cheering as he raised the blade high, a look of lust striking his wild eyes. "You *are* a failure, and as such you deserve to die!"

The guards who stood witness began to cheer and clap, their lust for a kill just as prevalent as Master Ito's. Mat hated them all.

But in defeat, for there was no way out of the situation

aside from a miracle, Mat hung his head. "Just do it, then. Kill me first, so I don't have to see Akai being taken from me. Give me that mercy at least."

"To the Kami of the temple," Master Ito began, kind of like a chant, "I give you this sacrifice to appease you for the one you were denied. Please accept it as you would have accepted the other." To Mat, eyes wide with lust, he said, "Now you'll receive your punishment, one that will last you for the rest of eternity."

To be continued…

About Kon Blacke

By day I'm a humble physical therapist...and by day I'm also a writer of sweet & saucy boyslove stories (18+). I sleep at night as an old fart like me should. I'm both self-published and traditionally published. Other than that, I live with my partner and two cats and live my best life.

Website: http://konblackeboyslovewriter.com

Twitter: http://www.twitter.com/blackekon

Books by Kon Blacke

Battle for Atashaal
A Cat's Play is the Death of Mice

The Legend of Hereward
Immortal Whispers (Book One)
Mortal Screaming (Book Two)

Boyslove in the Gangland District
Offering Gold Coins to a Cat (Book One)
Soft Boys Play Hard (Book Two)
Catching Two Frogs With One Hand (Book Three)
The Chirping Cricket Desires the Ripened Crop (Book Four)

The Saurian Love Trilogy
My Tyrannosaurus Lover (Book One)
My Saurian Friends (Book Two)

Shoju and Matashi
Warmth From the Rising Sun (Book One)
Cool From the Waxing Moon (Book Two)

Also by Kon Blacke
Published by Dreamsphere Books

Immortal Whispers
Kon Blacke

    The Whispering Monks have foretold change to the world, and it's fast approaching. They also speak of the mortals who'll be involved.

    Hereward, a lord knight who only worships the steel at his side, as the mad magician Ealdræd has taken away everyone he had ever loved. Wymond, an oblate determined to find his true self, even if it means turning away from everything he has ever known. Beornræd, a powerful magician who fears to love again after the cruelties of his past. Kieron, a stable hand with dragon blood flowing through his veins and is the rightful heir to a realm of unimaginable beauty.

    All four will travel their own paths, to destroy their pasts and rebuild their future, as they thwart the evil plans of Ealdræd and his conduit, the immortal Abbot Hosho.

    The whisperings continue through epic battles, both on the ground and in the sky.

    The whisperings shall continue beyond the aftermath.

    As it has been foretold.

Also by Kon Blacke

Offering Gold Coins to a Cat
Kon Blacke

Tachibana Kushano goes to Michael Brock's gentleman's club, Badda-Bings, to give himself to many other men at once. All because his boyfriend, Riyu, orders him to.

Tachibana never questions Riyu. He's his submissive, after all.

But when he's finished, Riyu still isn't happy, and Tachibana doesn't understand why. And as he quickly discovers, he's never been appreciated by Riyu either, even when he's done whatever he's been told without question. As a result of Riyu's anger, Tachibana is then punished, hurt beyond anything imaginable.

For Tachibana, it's the last straw.

The trouble is…how can he recover after being dominated by Riyu for so long? How can he learn to trust someone else again?

But above all, how can Tachibana love someone else, even someone who wants to care for him? Someone like Michael Brock, for instance?

Also by Kon Blacke

My Tyrannosaurus Lover
Kon Blacke

Karl Meddings is what you would call an ordinary guy in every way. He loves his best friend—with benefits—Sagan, with all his heart, and leads a good life. The only unusual thing about his world is the fact he shares it with saurians—the modern-day ancestors of dinosaurs.

But now, Karl's boss, a rather attractive tyrannosaurus by the name of Benedict Tumbold, has an interesting proposal for both Karl and Sagan—a proposal that could turn Karl from an ordinary guy with no real prospects to someone special.

A hero…

Will Karl accept his boss's offer? Will Sagan? Or will an ordinary life be all that Karl's destined for?

Printed in Great Britain
by Amazon

46700847R00088